Praise for the Kenni L

"Fabulous fun and fantastic fried mystery with another must-read mt. (Also, I want to live in Cottonwood, KY.) Don't miss this one!"

– Darynda Jones,
New York Times Bestselling Author of *Eighth Grave After Dark*

"Packed with clever plot twists, entertaining characters, and plenty of red herrings! *Fixin' To Die* is a rollicking, delightful, down-home mystery."

– Ann Charles,
USA Today Bestselling Author of the Deadwood Mystery Series

"Southern and side-splitting funny! *Fixin' To Die* has captivating characters, nosy neighbors, and is served up with a ghost and a side of murder."

– Duffy Brown,
Author of the Consignment Shop Mysteries

"This story offers up a small touch of paranormal activity that makes for a fun read...A definite "5-star," this is a great mystery that doesn't give up the culprit until the last few pages."

– *Suspense Magazine*

"A Southern-fried mystery with a twist that'll leave you positively breathless."

– Susan M. Boyer,
USA Today Bestselling Author of *Lowcountry Book Club*

"A wonderful series filled with adventure, a ghost, and of course some romance. This is a hard book to put down."

– Cozy Mystery Book Reviews

"Kappes captures the charm and quirky characters of small-town Kentucky in her new mystery…a charming, funny story with exaggerated characters. The dialect-filled quirky sayings and comments bring those characters to life."

– Lesa's Book Critiques

"With a fantastic cast of characters and a story filled with humor and murder you won't be able to put it down."

– Shelley's Book Case

"Funny and lively…Before you blink you're three chapters down and you're trying to peek ahead to see what happens next. Fast moving with great characters that you wish were real so that you might be able to visit with them more often."

– The Reading Room

"Kappes is an incredible author who weaves fabulous stories…I can't wait to see what she comes up next in this series."

– Community Bookstop

"I am totally hooked. The people of Cottonwood feel like dear friends, and I enjoy reading about the latest happenings…The story is well-told, with plenty of action and suspense, along with just enough humor to take the edge off."

– Book Babble

4

SIX FEET UNDER

**The Kenni Lowry Mystery Series
by Tonya Kappes**

SIX FEET UNDER

A KENNI LOWRY MYSTERY

UNDER

TONYA KAPPES

HENERY PRESS

Copyright

SIX FEET UNDER
A Kenni Lowry Mystery
Part of the Henery Press Mystery Collection

First Edition | March 2018

Henery Press, LLC
www.henerypress.com

All rights reserved. No part of this book may be used or reproduced in any manner whatsoever, including internet usage, without written permission from Henery Press, LLC, except in the case of brief quotations embodied in critical articles and reviews.

Copyright © 2018 by Tonya Kappes

This is a work of fiction. Any references to historical events, real people, or real locales are used fictitiously. Other names, characters, places, and incidents are the product of the author's imagination, and any resemblance to actual events or locales or persons, living or dead, is entirely coincidental.

Trade Paperback ISBN-13: 978-1-63511-308-2
Digital epub ISBN-13: 978-1-63511-309-9
Kindle ISBN-13: 978-1-63511-310-5
Hardcover ISBN-13: 978-1-63511-311-2

Printed in the United States of America

To Eddy:
ODO NNYEW FIE KWAN

Chapter One

"Y'all ain't gonna believe this" was the first thing Mama said as Finn Vincent and I moseyed into Ben's Diner. That was something you didn't want to hear out of Mama's mouth at seven in the morning. Or any time, for that matter.

"The clock is wrong?" I asked. "Because I know I'm not seeing you here at seven a.m."

Mama gave me the mom look. She quickly turned her attention to Duke, my fur-deputy bloodhound that went practically everywhere with me.

She bent down and patted him, letting him give her a few kisses. "You're never too old for a whoopin'." She looked up and wagged her finger at me.

The beating and banging coming from the other side of the diner caught my attention. The construction crew was already at it. And so early. I was going to need at least four cups of coffee instead of my usual two if Finn and I were going to be eating here.

"I know why we're here." I motioned between me and Finn, my deputy sheriff and recent boyfriend. Very recent. We were regular morning customers. "But why are you here so early? And looking fresh as a daisy?"

Mama stood up and brushed her hands together.

I looked at her closer and noticed her olive skin was a little too fresh. Her long brown hair was fixed as if she were heading to a party and her wrinkles were, um, less wrinkly. Maybe it was the beautiful spring morning we were having. The warm sunlight already beating through the windows of the diner projected on her and made her look a little more youthful.

"There is something going on with you." I pointed my finger in a circle around her head. "There's something wrong with her face." I turned to Finn.

Finn looked at me with a very amused expression. It was one of those curious looks that made my heart flip-flop every time he wore it. Over the past few months, we'd explored a relationship outside of the sheriff's office, and I'd have to say that it'd been going slowly but swimmingly.

"We're happy to see you this morning," Finn said, stepping between us and giving Mama a hug. He was using his new southern charm to do exactly that: charm my mama.

His voice was warm and deep, matching the depth of his eyes. His black hair was neatly combed to the side. The first time I'd seen him had been when the Kentucky Reserve Unit was called in to help on Doc Walton's murder investigation. I knew I was in trouble when my physical reaction to his presence was like nothing I'd ever experienced before. Now, a year later, he still had that same hold on me.

"It's refreshing to see your face instead of his," Finn said to Mama and playfully elbowed Ben Harrison, the owner of Ben's Diner, when he walked over to us with a couple of menus tucked up under his arm and three coffees.

He nodded his head towards our usual table up front near the window. Finn, Mama, Duke, and I followed him over.

"One for you." Ben set a coffee down in front of Finn. "Two for you." He sat the other two in front of me before he handed us the menus. "And something for you." Ben tugged a doggy treat out of the pocket of his jeans and gave it to Duke.

"New menus?" I asked, noticing the stained menus that were normally wedged between the salt and pepper shakers were no longer there. "New way of handing out the menus?"

"I was trying to tell you before you rudely interrupted." Mama pushed back over to me. "I'm sorry," she said to Finn. "I raised her better than that."

"Rude," Finn teased me, his smile making my breath catch.

He knew the tension between me and Mama had just started to dissolve in recent months after she'd finally accepted my career choice. I was the sheriff of our town, Cottonwood, Kentucky.

"I was saying that Frank Von Lee is going to be here today!" She bounced on her toes. "In a few short hours," she squealed.

"Really?" I asked a little louder than normal. The construction worker was making a bunch of ruckus banging on a new wood beam on the ceiling of the old building. "So soon? The diner doesn't look like it's completed yet." I turned around in my chair and gave the diner a good onceover.

Ben Harrison had been working hard over the past few months to get the diner camera ready for the Culinary Channel's show *Southern Home Cookin'*, starring the biggest southern culinary chef that'd turned food critic, Frank Von Lee.

"Yes." Mama clapped her hands together. "He's staying at the Tattered Cover Books and Inn right next door. They sure don't give you much notice. Glad I spruced up a bit." She pushed her manicured fingers into her hair to give it a little more volume.

"The diner will look great once they finish getting the beam up today and with a little elbow grease," Ben noted.

"This is it, Kenni." Mama beamed. "Winning that cooking contest last year and having my pot pie featured in the Cottonwood Chronicle has changed my life."

"Not to mention I added your delicious pot pie to our menu," Ben interrupted and pointed to the new menu, where it read "Cottonwood Chicken Pot Pie, homemade by Viv Lowry."

He called Mama by her nickname, short for Vivian.

"Mmhmm." Mama's lips were pressed tight as she hummed and nodded, pride all over her face. "That's me." Her shoulders drew up to her ears. Her nose curled, eyes squinted as she smiled. "I've gotten so much recognition." She talked to Finn like he didn't know what was going on.

"You deserve it too." Finn was good at feeding her ego.

"Do I look good?" She craned her neck side to side. "Which is my good side? Left or right?" She rotated some more.

There was definitely something going on with Mama's face. Maybe it was a lot of makeup.

"What?" Mama drew back and looked at me. "Do I have a booger?"

"No, Mama." I rolled my eyes.

"Both sides are beautiful, Viv." Finn was full of malarkey.

"Oh, Finn." Mama giggled and brushed her fingers towards him along with a nose scrunch.

She ran her hand over her hair and down her custom-made apron embroidered with her initials. "Edna is stopping by to do an exclusive interview with me this morning, and I've got to look my best." Edna Easterly was the Chronicle's reporter. Mama's face glowed with pride. "She's going to take some photos of me cooking my famous pot pie. She's going to come back tomorrow too, because that's when Frank is going to try the pot pie. But can you believe he's going to be here in a few short hours? We've been waiting so long for him."

"Frank? Since when are you on a first-name basis?" I asked, lowering my voice since the hammering had stopped.

Ben laughed.

"It's not guaranteed that I'm going to make it on the show." She let out a deep sigh. "There is that diner over in Clay's Ferry he's going to later in the week." She tossed a loose wave of hair. "It's between me and them." She swung her finger back and forth between us. "But you and I both know I'm going to win." She winked.

The construction worker passed us with some wood propped up on his shoulder.

"I'm sorry about the mess. He should be out of here in an hour." Ben let out a deep sigh. "I was hoping to get the whole diner remodeled, but we just ran out of time."

Ben looked exhausted. He had on his normal baseball cap turned backward over his shaggy brown hair. It didn't matter if the president was coming, he wouldn't stray from his normal plaid-shirt-and-jeans look.

"A whistling woman and a crowing hen never come to a very good end." The faint whisper of a familiar voice breezed past my ear.

Duke jumped up and wagged his tail.

"A whistling woman and a crowing hen never come to a very good end," I repeated in a hushed tone, looking around to see exactly where the familiar voice of the ghost of my Poppa was coming from.

My stomach dropped. The room tilted slightly and I grabbed the edges of the diner table.

"Hey there, Kenni-bug," Poppa greeted me in a long, low voice, stretching out the greeting. "I'm back."

Chapter Two

"What did you just say?" Mama asked. Her body stiffened.

"A whistling woman and a crowing hen never come to a very good end." My Poppa's ghost did a little jig on his way over to the table with a big grin on his face. He clapped his thick hands in delight.

Duke shimmied and shook with excitement. His nails moved along the diner's tile floor as Poppa danced around.

"Well?" Mama planted her hand on the table and leaned in towards me. "I'm waiting."

"What is Duke doing?" Finn's head tilted to the side.

I cleared my throat and reached over, grabbing Duke by the collar.

"He's probably hungry," I lied, ignoring Mama.

The diner was starting to fill up with the breakfast rush crowd. The way I saw it was that if I did repeat the expression as Mama asked me to do, there were too many people around for her to pitch a fit. Mama would never let anyone see her lose her religion in public, because it wasn't pretty. I'd been on the receiving end of it, and it was nothing I'd wish on my worst enemy.

"I asked you to repeat what you said," Mama demanded through gritted teeth.

"A whistling woman and a crowing hen never come to a very good end," I choked out.

"Where did you hear that?"

"Yeah, before I died, I used to say that to your mama all the time." Poppa had a way of playing little jokes on me since I was the only one who could see and hear him. "Good boy." He patted Duke on the head.

It'd been a little over three years since he died. Elmer Sims had been the sheriff of Cottonwood and my mama's daddy. He was my rock and I looked up to him more than anyone else in this world. Something Mama had a problem with, especially after I went to the police academy and ran for sheriff of Cottonwood, where I was now in my third year of a four-year term.

Thank God the bell over the front door jingled, signaling someone's entrance, because it took the heat off of me. It was Edna, here to do Mama's interview for the Cottonwood Chronicle.

"Mornin', Sheriff." She nodded my way. The bright orange feather hot-glued to the side of her yellow fedora waved in the air with the swoosh of the door closing behind her. "You ready to get this show on the road, Viv?"

Edna stuck her hand in her usual fisherman's vest where she kept all her writing utensils and took out a pen and paper.

She gave a finger wave to Mama and pointed toward the counter before she walked across the diner and sat down on one of the stools next to the regulars. She didn't give anyone but Mama eye contact. She was focused. There wasn't anything that required such media attention that I knew of, if you could call the Cottonwood Chronicle media. Besides the Chronicle, we did have a small radio station in town, WCKK, that played oldies and did a few interviews with citizens in Cottonwood.

"I'm not done with you yet." Mama shook a finger at me. "I'm going to do my interview, but I want an answer when I get back. I've not heard that expression in a long time and I know I've never said it in front of you." Her tongue was sharp. "And don't forget about my class tonight at Lulu's Boutique. I expect you to be there."

Poppa smacked his thigh and doubled over laughing. He stood next to Finn, who was sitting across from me looking at the menu. He'd gotten used to ignoring Mama's and my banter. Only this time, she meant business.

"I won't forget." I confirmed that I would at the cooking class she was offering to the community.

It had been a little over a year ago when the ghost of my Poppa showed up after two simultaneous crimes were committed in Cottonwood. Before that, there hadn't been any crime on my watch since I'd taken office two years prior. It wasn't until I'd accepted the fact that Poppa was my guardian angel deputy from the great beyond that I realized he'd been scaring away any would-be criminals during those first two years of my term. Since then, whenever Poppa showed up, I knew there was some sort of crime about to happen. Though I loved seeing him, it made me feel sick to know the reason he was here.

"What can I get you to eat? Your usual?" Ben asked.

"Coffee is fine." I'd suddenly lost my appetite. There was no way I was going to be able to stomach a thing before talking to Poppa to find out exactly why he was here.

Finn looked up at me and narrowed his eyes.

"You were starving before we got here. What's going on with you?" he asked.

It was cute how his voice held concern when just a few short months ago he probably wouldn't have noticed if I'd not eaten. We'd been spending more and more time together in the off hours since he'd moved in down the street.

"Nothing." I turned my attention to Ben. "The diner looks great. I love how you're replacing the old wood beams with new ones."

"Thanks." He pointed to the old wooden ceiling. "The beams really needed to be redone, and even though Frank Von Lee is only here to taste the pot pie to decide if they will feature it on the show, I thought I'd go ahead and get the work done anyways."

"I don't blame you. Y'all deserve to be recognized for all this amazing southern food." I smiled. "What are you trying to finish in a couple of hours?"

"I got the floors buffed and shined. He's on the last beam now. The menus are done, and all I have left is getting a new pot holder to replace the old one hanging above the kitchen island." Ben rocked back on the heels of his shoes.

"It looks great so far," I assured my friend.

The door between the kitchen and the dining room swung open and smacked up against the wall. The bang got everyone's attention real fast. The chatter among the guests stopped and all eyes watched as the man who emerged from the kitchen stalked over to Ben.

"I can't work in this atmosphere." The man, wearing a white chef jacket, dragged a white cap off of his head. His brown hair was matted down and wet from sweat. "This is not how I imagined this would be. I expected a quiet work environment for perfection. Not destruction. I cannot and will not work in this...this mess!"

Out of the corner of my eye, I saw Poppa ghost himself gone.

"Yes, you will." Ben's face turned crimson with fury. "You're the one who said you'd love to do the job since we knew each other and graduated from culinary school together. You jumped at the chance. You signed a contract. I paid you upfront and you won't make a fool out of this diner or me. You and I both know you need this job, so you aren't going anywhere. Do you understand?" Ben jabbed the man in between his shoulder and collarbone. The man took a step back in a vicious jerk. His eyes narrowed to crinkled slits.

The man stomped off in the direction of the kitchen.

Ben offered us an apology. "I had to hire Mundy to run the diner while I took care of the construction. I can't be everything around here."

Ben Harrison had a couple of locals that helped in the diner here and there, mainly high school kids to bus and clean, but otherwise, it was just him running the entire place. He had done all the cooking up until now.

"This is why I've always been hesitant to hire people." He offered an apologetic smile.

"No worries, man." Finn shrugged it off. "This Frank seems to be a big deal. I'm sure everyone is a little tense today."

My focus was on Ben. I'd known him all my life and I'd never seen him get so angry.

"Now, what is this about you not being hungry?" Ben asked and changed the subject.

"I'm just going to have my coffee for now." I wrapped my hand around one of the white ceramic mugs to warm them from the chill of nerves that were shooting through my body.

"Fine." Finn handed the new menu back to Ben. "I'm going to have the Cottonwood special."

"Great choice." Ben took the menu. "It's a new one, along with the hot brown for supper. You'll have to come back tomorrow during the tasting so the diner will be full when Frank Von Lee is here. I want a good showing, ya know."

"Absolutely," Finn agreed. I nodded too.

"By the looks of this morning, you're going to have standing room only." I was proud of my friend. He'd come a long way from the grilled cheese we'd made in my mama's kitchen when we were in high school and pulling all-nighters studying.

"Two more won't hurt," he said.

After a few more minutes of chitchat, Ben headed back to the cranky new chef, leaving Finn and me alone. Finn waited until Ben walked off to reach across the table and touch my hand. The warmth of his touch made me tingle. My pulse quickened and my tear ducts swelled.

"Are you okay?" he asked. "You look like you're in another world."

Another world? The afterlife. My stomach churned. If only Finn knew about Poppa.

I licked my lips. Was it time I told my real partner about my ghost partner? Before I could say a word, his cell phone buzzed on the table. He pulled his hand off mine and I watched as he picked it up to look at the number.

"I'm sorry." Finn stood up. "I need to take this." A look of irritation washed over his face after he pressed the phone up to his ear and headed out of the diner to talk in private.

I blinked the tears from my eyes and flipped my attention to my mama. Edna's eye was pressed up against her camera, clicking away as Mama posed in the strangest positions with an empty casserole dish, a spatula, and a big ole smile on her face.

Poppa appeared next to Mama. I covered my mouth with my hand and laughed, watching him mimic Mama. It was so good to see him, but I was also waiting for the other shoe to drop when Poppa came and a crime hadn't been reported.

"Sorry about that." Finn stood next to his chair.

"Cottonwood special." Ben sat the plate in front of Finn.

My mouth watered at the sight of the special. The Cottonwood special was goetta sausage, cheddar jack cheese, and sautéed onions baked in a mini cast-iron skillet with a fried egg on top.

"That was my contractor." Finn sat back down. "I'm having the hardest time getting the construction done on the house. This is the second time they've canceled." Finn shook his head.

The house Finn had bought from Lonnie Lemar, my old deputy, had been a rental property for Lonnie. Like most rentals, there was a lot of work that needed to be done after the tenants moved out. Finn decided to put a little addition on the back, connecting the family room and kitchen into one big room.

"They've been doing this addition for months now. I'm going to have to find someone else." He let out a long exhausted sigh. "He said he's too busy to finish the job but still wants to be paid for what they've done."

"Who did you use?" Ben asked and set down a to-go cup of coffee on the table for me. It was so nice to have a good friend who knew exactly what I needed.

"Danny Shane." The local building company consisted of Danny and his three sons. Finn rolled his eyes.

"Yeah. Damn shame, ain't it? His family has spent decades building up their construction business. Danny takes over and they go to hell in a hand basket," Ben said, catching my attention. "I fired him a couple of days ago, and luckily these guys were in here when it happened and they do construction, so I hired them and they're getting it done." Ben shook a finger at me. "You know what, I'm glad I fired him. Someone told me Danny said my food gave him food poisoning. Jerk."

Ben had never been so on edge. It had to be because of the stress of the food critic's visit. After all, it would be his diner that would take the hit, not necessarily Mama. Her ego might be bruised if she wasn't picked. That'd be on me to listen to for years.

"A couple of days ago?" Finn chuckled. "They shouldn't be busy then and should've been able to come by the house."

"Riley," Ben hollered and snapped his wrist in a wave at one of the construction guys to come over. "Finn Vincent, this is Riley Titan. Amazing man who did all this work."

The two men shook hands.

"Riley, Finn is in the same boat I was in with the same contractor. Do you think you can run over to his house on Broadway and take a look at his addition?" Ben asked.

"I'm not going to do this!" the chef screamed from the pass-through window into the diner. He flung the towel off his shoulder and threw it down.

"I'm going to knock him in the head with a rolling pin." Ben's jaw tensed. He turned on a dime and stalked back to the kitchen.

"Is it okay if I head over tonight?" Riley asked.

He was a little overweight and sweat beaded along his forehead under his shaggy head of hair. He looked around thirty and a little too young to be so out of shape.

"After six is great." Finn wrote down his address on a paper napkin. After Riley walked away, Finn said, "I guess I better go visit Danny and settle up on what I owe him."

"Yeah. I better go make my rounds." I looked down at Duke. "Ready, Duke?"

He jumped to his feet, eager to go. He loved going for rides.

"I'll talk to you soon." Finn gave me a kiss goodbye and Duke a good scratch behind his ear before he left.

On my way out the door, I glanced back at Mama. Her lips were flapping a mile a minute as Edna wrote just as fast. Poppa was nowhere to be seen. Even as my foot stepped over the threshold, the sound of pans banging around and yelling came from the kitchen.

"I'm telling you that I'm not going to work in this noise. It hinders my creative flow and I'm not going to do it. Contract or not!" Mundy, the temporary chef, shuffled backwards in front of the pass-through kitchen window.

When I saw Ben practically chasing him, I hurried back through the diner, but not without noticing everyone was either sitting and watching or walking back to see what was going on.

Even Mama's interview had come to a halt. Duke had already made it to the kitchen before I'd even gotten close. It wasn't unusual for my furry sidekick to rush in before me. He'd even taken a bullet for me a few months ago and got a medal from the town because of it.

"All right. Break it up." I pushed through the door to find Mundy jabbing a big sharp knife towards Ben.

Riley was hanging out on top of the ladder with a DeWalt drill in his hand where he'd been hanging the new pot holder over the island. Slowly he eased down each rung and ducked back into the diner. I didn't blame him. The knife Mundy was swinging at Ben could possibly fly out of the crazed man's hand, and who knew where it'd land.

Neither man bothered to look at me. Duke tried to get between them because he knew they couldn't resist a cute dog.

"You will hold up your end of the deal!" Ben screamed back at him. His jaw tensed, his fist balled at his side. I could feel the anger coming from him. Then he released a finger to swipe it across Duke's head because Duke wouldn't stop nudging his leg.

Ben took the tea towel off his shoulder and wound it around his hand as he tried to grab the knife. Duke stuck to him like a booger on a finger. "Duke, shoo."

Ben lifted his leg to try to get Duke to move, but the dog didn't budge. It was like he knew that Ben needed to calm down, just like I knew he had to knock it off.

"All right!" I had to scream over the two men again. "That's it. Break it up." I did that whole cop stance thing with my legs apart and rested my hand on the butt of my gun nestled in my belt holster. "I'm thinking this employment is over or I can take both of you to the office."

Not that I had to go far. My office was just a few doors down in the back room of Cowboy's Catfish. If I did have to haul them down, I really wasn't sure what I'd do with one of them since we only had one cell. There wasn't any way they'd be able to stay in there. They'd for sure kill each other. Another murder wasn't anything I, or Cottonwood, needed.

Mundy looked at me, his nostrils flaring with his deep inhale. His eyes slid over to Ben, who was still leveling a death stare at the poor man. His chest heaved up and down, and his mouth twitched.

Mundy set the knife down on the counter and put his hands in the air.

"I don't want no trouble. I just want to leave," he said to me.

"Fine. If you have any belongings, grab them and we'll wait right here." I was glad to see things come to an end without someone getting a finger chopped off.

"That's my knife." He went to get it, but I made an eh-eh noise to shoo him away. "Chefs carry their own knives. Besides, I wouldn't've wasted a good sharpened knife on the likes of him." The right corner of his lip snarled.

Ben didn't move, even when Duke tried to get him to rub his head. Duke had even gone as far as putting the top of his head in Ben's dangling hand, but Ben was stiff.

The chef didn't take long. He had a cloth bag rolled up in his hands with his knives in it.

"I swear you are dead," Ben said through gritted teeth when the chef walked past him to get out of the diner. "No one in this industry will hire you ever again."

Ben couldn't leave well enough alone.

The chef stopped so they were shoulder to shoulder. His chin glided toward Ben. Their eyes met. I took a step forward, but the chef hocked a big loogie at Ben's feet before he walked out.

The clicks from Edna's fancy camera clicked at rapid speed.

She sure did have a front-page story for tomorrow's edition.

"Sonofa…" Ben grumbled. He took off his hat and threw it on the ground.

"What is wrong with you?" I interrupted him. "We've known each other since we were knee-high babies and I've never seen you act like such a loon."

He dragged the toe of his shoe back and forth before he bent down and picked up his hat. Duke saw this as his opportunity to get in a lick since Ben was at his eye level. Ben's hand finally gave in to the very determined bloodhound. Duke stretched out in delight with each scratch of Ben's nails.

He shook his head and dragged his hand up to his hair, raking his fingers through it.

The stress had taken a toll on him. The wrinkles next to his eyes had deepened. The bags under his eyes had darkened.

"It just so happened that Mundy called me yesterday right after I'd made a decision to hire someone while I took the extra time to get the work on the diner completed. No sooner did I get off the phone with him than the Culinary Channel called to let me know Frank was coming today. Mundy was working up at Le Fork where we'd met in school. I called him back and offered him the job with a contract. Sight unseen, he took the job and showed up here today." He threw his hands up in the air. "He was always a great chef. I even made it easy on him by letting him have free creative expression while Viv and I focused on her pot pie."

"Now it's over and we need to move on. I'm sure you'll think of something. You always do." I could tell by the expression on his face that he didn't give two cents what I was saying. "He did seem like a hot head, so maybe it's a good thing he's gone before Frank gets here."

That sounded like a bright side to me.

While Ben had been doing his culinary thing, I was off to

the police academy. During that time I rarely kept up with my old friend from high school. I just wanted to get through my training and get out. It wasn't until Poppa died that I'd decided to come back, which was when I'd reconnected with my childhood friends.

"He can go back to Le Fork up in Lexington. Granted, Ben's is a step down from his big restaurant dreams." Ben shook his head. "I knew better. He's ruined every place he's ever gone. I was giving him a shot."

"Some people just don't know a good thing when they see one. Plus, how well can he cook your cornbread?" I tried to offer sympathy with my voice. Southern cooking truly was an art form. Some people thought we just threw things in a fryer. Not true. It was the golden crisp, just enough lard, and the perfect seasonings that made my mouth water with every dish at Ben's.

"What am I going to do with just a few hours left before Frank Von Lee gets here?" Ben asked.

I would've offered my services, but no one in Cottonwood wanted a frozen dinner from the Dixon's Foodtown.

My phone chirped a text. It was from Jolee Fischer, my best friend and Ben's girlfriend.

"I need a friend to talk to. Ben's all nuts and crazy over this Frank thing and we've not spent any time together."

"I think I just solved your chef problem." I quickly texted Jolee, "Where are you?"

She replied, "On my way to park the food truck at Lulu's."

Jolee owned the only food truck in Cottonwood, On The Run. Every day she parked her truck in different locations around the city. Most mornings she parked in front of Lulu's Boutique on the north side of town so the people going to work in town could stop for a quick breakfast sandwich and coffee.

"Can you stop by Ben's Diner first?" I wrote.

"Sure thing."

"What do you mean you think you solved my problem?" Ben asked.

It was a perfect solution. "Think about it. Jolee and you haven't been spending a lot of time together. She would love to help you out. She can get Viola White and Myrna Savage to take over since they were the runners-up against Mama."

It was a brilliant idea.

"It's only two days that Frank will be here." I continued to sell him on the idea. "You know she can cook good food too. And without you watching over her."

"I think this might work." The smiling Ben I'd known all my life appeared before me with a very thankful face. "One more thing. Can you come here this afternoon and do crowd control? According to the latest phone call, Frank wants to come here after he checks in and talk to me and Viv."

"No problem. I'll be back in a few hours." I patted my leg for Duke to come. "Jolee will be here in a minute. You can discuss the situation with her because I've got to do my morning drive-bys."

Duke and I headed out the door. My shoulders were back and I was confident that I'd just kept the peace once again in Cottonwood. Though there was the one little issue that had just showed up. Poppa.

Chapter Three

After doing my morning rounds and stopping to say hello to a few of the citizens walking around, I headed on back to the office to see what was going on there. All seemed to be quiet and I'd not seen hide nor hair of Poppa.

Betty Murphy, my office clerk and dispatch operator, was busy filing and answering the phones. I typed a little report up about what had gone on at Ben's Diner just in case it came back to bite me in the hiney. One aspect of the sheriff's job was to document everything. This would be classified as disturbing the peace.

The dispatch phone rang. Betty scurried over to answer it, probably thankful for the distraction from answering any more of my questions. I flipped Duke a treat from the jar that sat on my desk.

"Dispatch, how can I help you?" Betty asked in her sweet southern drawl. "Why, hello, Viv."

My head jerked up.

I waved my hands in the air and shook my head at Betty. She looked up at me and smiled. "I'm not here," I whispered.

"Why, she sure is here. No, she's not busy at all. Hold on." Betty clicked the hold button. "Sheriff, your mama is on line one."

I eyeballed her.

"I'm not lying to your mama." She didn't look at me. She busied herself with some papers on her desk.

A bigger sigh than normal escaped my body so Betty would know I wasn't happy with her ignoring me.

I picked up the receiver, pushed the button, and said, "Hello, Mama."

"I found out what restaurant he's going to in Clay's Ferry." There was excitement in her voice.

I should've known Mama wasn't going to let it go. She had an itch to find out what diner she was competing against and she scratched it.

"Betty said you weren't busy, so I'm going to head over to the department and get you and take you to lunch," Mama said. "We have a couple more hours until Frank gets here."

There she went calling him Frank again as if she knew him personally.

"Mama, I'm knee deep in paperwork. I need to get it done. Maybe another day." I thought my excuse was a pretty good one for thinking on my feet, which was hard to do when I was talking to her. She always seemed to fluster me.

"We have to go on what you'd call a stakeout." There was an uptick in her tone that I didn't like.

"Stakeout?" I laughed. "No. I'm not going on no stakeout," I assured her.

"Fine. Then how about lunch with your mama." She wasn't going to let it go that I didn't have anything to do. "We can go wherever you want. I'm nervous. I need my daughter."

And there went the guilt she was good at. What was a lunch date with her going to hurt? After all, she'd worked really hard to get the visit from Frank Von Lee. She'd won a local cooking competition between Jolee Fischer's food truck and Ben's Diner. Mama's chicken pot pie won and somehow the Culinary Channel found out and it was all she wrote after that. The least I could do was go eat with her.

"Wherever I want?" I asked. "Is there a catch?"

"Can't a mama take her only daughter out to lunch?" she asked. "After all, later I'm going to be busy with Frank in town and then the filming."

Mama had a big ego. She'd already proclaimed herself the winner of the spot on the Culinary Channel before the contest had even begun.

"All right." There was no sense in arguing with her. Everyone in Cottonwood knew that what Viv Lowry wanted, Viv Lowry got. "I'll even let you pick where we eat."

There was a nigglin' suspicion that Mama was suddenly feeling generous and it was at my expense. But I was willing to play along just to see exactly what she had up her sleeve.

Chapter Four

I'd decided to leave Duke at the office with Betty. Not that she'd mind. I knew she'd have to get up and take him out, but she liked getting out in the community and talking to the neighbors. It was good as dispatcher to be known in town. Especially with the election coming up. Luckily, I was running unopposed, though that could change on a dime. I didn't put anything past the people of Cottonwood.

I'd made sure everyone in and around Cottonwood stayed happy with the department. Seeing Poppa this morning was wonderful but meant something was stirring in Cottonwood. That was bad. At least, that'd been the pattern before. When he showed up, there was either a murder or a robbery.

Mama pulled up in her big white Escalade. Her eyes barely reached the top of the steering wheel.

"You want me to drive?" I asked, hoping she'd agree, but Mama never let anyone drive. Not even Daddy. Ever. Poor Daddy.

"Nope." Once I was settled in the passenger seat, she flung the gearshift into drive and headed down the alley.

At the stop sign, she dragged her head side to side to look both ways. I noticed the lines on her face were practically gone.

"Mama?" I asked when she leaned way over the steering wheel to see across me. I pushed my back into the leather seat. "What on earth has happened to your face?"

"What on earth are you talking about, Kendrick?" Mama

saying my full name was a surefire way of knowing she didn't want to answer the question.

"I don't know." I gripped the door handle when she punched the gas, pulling right out in front of Doolittle Bowman's car on West Walnut Street. She was able to turn the wheel and push the electric window button at the same time. I feared for my life and held on tighter.

"That's my girl. Woo wee!" Poppa yelped from the back.

"Thank you!" Mama screamed and threw her hand out the window as if Doolittle had stopped and graciously let Mama out. Which she didn't.

I looked at the side mirror and Doolittle was giving Mama two kinds of hell. Good thing I wasn't able to read lips because she was giving Mama the business and honking her horn.

"Mama, you pulled out in front of her." I sucked in a deep breath.

"Honey, there was plenty of room. I'm sure she sped up when she saw me pulling out. That's the way them Bowmans are." Mama tilted her chin up as if she'd done nothing wrong.

"That's right, Viv." Poppa proudly stated from the backseat. I refrained from turning around because Mama would think I was looking at Doolittle, whose front bumper was practically kissing Mama's back bumper.

When Mama turned right on Main Street, my mind turned over, trying to think of any restaurants Mama would privy herself to eat in on that side of town.

"Where're we going to eat?" I asked Mama.

"Now don't be going and having a dying duck fit."

"Trigger word," I grumbled, knowing that this was no mother/daughter lunch to just chitchat about life.

"What do you mean trigger word?" Sarcasm dripped in Mama's honey-sweet southern accent.

"Whenever I questioned anything you did when I was at

home or there was something I wasn't going to enjoy doing, you'd say 'Kenni, don't be going and having a dying duck fit.'" I tried my best to do her accent and tone.

"That's not how I sound," Mama shot back.

"Pretty darn good if you ask me." Poppa cackled from the back.

I'm not gonna lie, I huffed and puffed a little. A duck fit might have been brewing up in me.

"Tell me what's in that pea-pickin' brain of yours." I was tired of playing games.

"Well..." She dragged the word out.

"Now, Mama," I said through gritted teeth.

"I've decided to take you to a nice little diner over in Clay's Ferry." She pushed the pedal a little faster as she passed the city limits sign on the far end of town.

"Mama, no," I responded. "You're going to your competition."

"Competition?" Mama laughed. "What have I told you all your life, Kendrick Lowry? We are in competition with no one. We are leaders."

"Poor, poor souls." I prayed for the people we were about to encounter. They'd no idea what the wrath of Mama was like.

This was Mama's pattern. Way back when I was five and entered the pig catching contest at our annual festival, she'd made sure she'd scared all the other kids, telling them about biting pigs, so that when it was time for me to run in the muddy area to catch the pig, I was the only contestant. Then in high school when I was running for student council, she'd offered the mothers of the other candidates a place on the Cottonwood Beautification Committee if their child withdrew from the election. But when it came to running for sheriff my first time, she'd done everything in her power to sabotage me, even went as far as putting in Duke as a write-in.

After I won, she'd sort of accepted the fact that I was an adult and making my own choices. Then, a few months ago when retired deputy Lonnie Lemar decided to run against me in the next election, Mama Bear came out and she pinned a Vote for Lowry pin on anything that she could.

Thankfully Lonnie ended up having a few issues in his personal life that gave him back his God-given sense and he pulled out of the race, leaving me with no competition...yet.

That made Mama happy, because even though she didn't like me being sheriff, she liked losing less. So she'd decided to let me put my life on the line for the sake of saying we won.

"What are you babbling about?" Mama's nose curled.

"Fascinating." I leaned closer to Mama as she bounced us up, down, and around the hills of the back roads toward Clay Ferry. "Even when you crinkle your nose, your lines still aren't visible."

"Shush your mouth, Kendrick." Mama pulled her shoulders back. "I figured we'd just go eat lunch. No one will know we're there. It's healthy to go and check out your competition."

I smacked my hands together. Mama jumped. She scowled again.

I took another look at Mama's flawless face. "You've had some work done on your face."

Why hadn't I thought of that earlier?

"What are you talking about?" Mama held the wheel steady as she sped up.

"You know exactly what I'm talking about. Botox? Filler? I bet you're the first person in Cottonwood to get a facelift." I knew I'd get her goat.

"Facelift? No such thing." Mama dragged the pad of her finger up to the corner of her eye and tapped it a little. "I just had a little plumping done so when I go on camera, I'm not all saggy."

"Mama," I gasped. "I can't believe you did this."

"What?" She drew back. "Kenni, it's national TV."

"You've lost your ever-loving mind. Poor Daddy. I hope he makes it through these next couple of days." I shook my head.

I shouldn't have been surprised. It was just like Mama to try to one-up people before they even knew they were one-upped by her. This was her specialty. Her southern manners were spot on. It was too late when you realized Mama was getting her way no matter what.

"Enough of that. What did you think about Ben's today?" Mama was good at changing the subject.

"For starters, I'm not sure why he's gone and done all this work on the diner. Its oddness was what made it so special. Don't get me wrong, your pot pie is phenomenal, but Ben's trying to change everything when really the focus is on you," I said.

"Chef Mundy wasn't nice." Mama's lip twitched. "He said he'd made better pot pie than me and he even tried to make one."

"He did?" My brows furrowed. Mama nodded. "I'm surprised you didn't whack him."

"I almost did. Luckily Ben put him in his place by telling him that the Culinary Channel was there to see me and he was there to cook the rest of the orders. The chef didn't like that." She shrugged. "I'm glad he's gone."

I looked at the speedometer and noted the Clay's Ferry county line was coming up soon.

"I'm glad for Jolee. She said Ben's crazy attitude has really taken a toll on their new relationship. Slow down, Mama," I said. "Their sheriff isn't as nice as me."

"Speaking of sheriff…" She held the wheel with her left hand and reached into her backseat.

"What on earth are you doing?" My tone escalated. "Keep

both hands on the wheel."

"Here." She threw a duffle bag of mine next to me on the front seat. "I took the liberty of getting you some regular clothes from your house to put on while we went to lunch. They can't know we're from Cottonwood and your uniform screams it."

"Remind me to take your key away." I unzipped the bag and tugged on the sweater over my uniform shirt. Mama didn't care; she came into my house no matter what time of day it was.

"And put a little lipstick on too. It'll make you feel better." Mama's cure for everything was lipstick.

"I don't feel bad," I said.

"You probably will after you eat this food." Mama pulled into The Little Shack barbeque joint's parking lot.

Chapter Five

The Little Shack was one of those barbeque joints that you would drive by a few hundred times and wonder how on earth someone could eat in there. The shotgun establishment needed a new siding job or a good scrubbing and a fresh coat of paint. The OPEN sign only blinked the letter P. Even the parking lot needed a good overhaul. The once-concrete pavement was now in chunks.

"Hold on." Mama gripped the wheel and bumped the car up to the front of the door in the handicap parking spot.

Surely she wasn't going to park here, I thought to myself, but then she put the gearshift into park.

"Mama, I don't know exactly what you've done to your face, but it's messed up your eyesight." I jutted my finger toward the faded handicap sign. "Handicap, Mama."

She leaned her body over the front seat and opened the glovebox. She grabbed a handicap hanger and slapped it around the rearview mirror.

"What on earth?" I took a closer look at the tag. The wheelchair was pink. "Is this real?"

I never took a good look at the tags before; I just gave tickets to cars parked in the handicap spots with no tag in the window or on the license plate.

"Of course it's real or I wouldn't have it." She reached behind the seat and grabbed her pocketbook. She started to get out of the car. "I told you that I got a little plumping, so I'm delicate for a couple of weeks. That's all."

I hollered out to her before she got out and had the opportunity to slam the door. "Did plumping make you lose your brain? You're not handicapped."

"Unless they changed it for gender color, that isn't real." Poppa had ghosted himself into Mama's seat and he too took a nice long look at it. "Maybe I'm here because your mama has lost her marbles. It does run in the family."

"You don't think Mama is going to..." I gulped, wondering if Poppa was like the ferryman to the underworld and he was here to collect Mama.

He shrugged.

I jumped out of the car.

"Oh, Mama." I grabbed her and kissed her cheek. "I love you so much. Are you sick?"

"Sick?" She pushed me away. "You seem to be the one with something wrong." She twisted around on the balls of her feet and trotted into The Little Shack with her pocketbook swinging in the crook of her arm. "You need to mind your own P's and Q's."

Poppa took notice too. He made sure he stayed next to her the entire time we were there.

"Take a seat," the woman behind the cash register next to the door hollered out but never looked up.

"Welcome to The Shack," a man from the kitchen window yelled and dinged the bell resting on the ledge.

Mama helped herself to one of the middle picnic tables. There were five picnic tables perpendicular to the door and two running along both sides of the wall to help accommodate the small shotgun of the building.

"Mama, remember, we're just here to taste the food." I nodded, hoping to shut down any thoughts in her head.

"Y'all want a coke or water?" the woman from the register

asked.

She'd moseyed over and pulled an ink pen from her messy brown updo.

"Where's your notepad?" Mama asked in a curt way.

"I don't need no notepad." The woman's accent was much more hick than ours.

You'd find that in Kentucky. You could drive two hours north of here and not hear a bit of a southern accent. You could drive two miles south of here and everyone sounded like they were from the far south.

"Hm." Mama pursed her lips. "This doesn't seem all that nice."

The woman let out a long sigh and leaned on her right side with her hip cocked out.

"I'll have a sweet tea." Mama straightened her shoulders as if she were in the front pew of Cottonwood Baptist Church on display for all to see.

"Coke or water," the woman repeated and took the pen, scribbling something on the white paper tablecloth.

"Is it tap or bottled?"

The woman stared down her nose at Mama, none too happy.

"We'll each have a coke," I suggested the best bet. The woman sauntered off in no big hurry to get us the cokes.

"I don't drink coke. I drink tea," Mama protested like a little child.

"She never did like coke," Poppa backed her up.

"If I didn't say coke, she'd have gotten you some toilet water because you are acting as if you are too good to be in here." I curled my fingers together and placed them in front of me, leaning on my forearms. "You've got to go unnoticed. If someone finds out who you are..." Mama's brows furrowed. She didn't get it. I shook my head and tried again. "If they find out that we're here to see your competition, we won't be welcome. Now act normal."

Inwardly I groaned, knowing this was her normal.

"Let's talk about your face." I had to bring it back up. I was in a state of shock over it. "What did you do?"

"I might've had a little work done so I'll look good on camera when they film the segment." Mama lifted her chin and dragged her fingers along her jaw. "A little tightening here." She moved them up to her crow's feet. "A little filler here. Maybe a little plump up here." She tapped her lips.

"Why on earth would you do that?" I questioned. "You are Viv Lowry. You don't need any help."

"Honey, we all need help." Her eyes assessed me. "Tomorrow it will look better and in a week when they film, it'll look natural."

Mama and I sat back enough to give the waitress some room to put the cokes down.

"What do you want?" she asked.

"Where's the menu?" Mama crossed her arms.

"Right down there." The woman pointed to the white paper tablecloth she'd written on that we hadn't paid attention to. "Pulled pork, pulled beef, pulled chicken. All barbeque. French fries, hush puppies, and coleslaw."

Mama curled her nose.

"I guess I'll have the chicken." Not a fan of the menu display, Mama put her finger in the air.

"What's she doing?" Poppa asked with concern. "Tell her to put her finger down."

"One suggestion," Mama started.

"Mama," I warned, but it was too late.

"You could use a little help on your menu writing skills. You are very sloppy and people can't read that. You could also explain what you are doing. I thought you'd contaminated my eating space."

"Is that so?" The woman shifted her eyes from Mama to me.

I smiled an empathetic smile.

"Honey, you're the one with her, not me." The woman had a point.

Mama's tight plumped-up bottom lip dropped.

"I'll have the chicken too. It sounds good." I said and whacked Mama under the table with my foot before Mama had any opportunity to say another word.

"What did you do that for?" Mama yelped and reached down to rub her shin.

"Two chicks!" the waitress called and walked back to the register.

I looked around to see who she was calling out to, but no one seemed to be looking at her or us for that matter. The place was packed and three new people had joined us at our picnic table.

"You eat here before?" Mama questioned the man next to her.

"Best barbeque in the state." The man smiled. "In fact, they are going to be featured on the Culinary Channel."

"Not if I have anything to do with it," Mama grumbled under her breath and turned from the man. The man's brows dipped and he scoffed at Mama. Again, I gave another sympathetic smile.

Whether she knew him or not, he'd said fighting words and Mama was a grudge holder. Shocker.

"I think that stuff," I circled my finger around her face, "has gone into your brain and messed you up. Where are your manners?"

Mama crossed her arms and ignored me by looking around. She couldn't deny it was clean and really kinda cute with the whole barbeque theme that went so well with the picnic décor.

My stomach did a flip-flop. If the food was as good as it smelled, Mama's pot pie might be in trouble.

The waitress walked over with a plastic basket filled to the brim with barbequed pulled chicken, crispy hushpuppies, crinkle fries, and creamy coleslaw. My mouth watered.

"Plastic?" Mama was no fan of plastic. She believed in using fine china for everything. Her motto was to use it if you had it.

"This is just one step up from paper." Mama took her plastic fork and rolled it into the chicken. She put her nose down into it and took a big whiff. "Too much barbeque sauce."

There wasn't anything good about it according to Mama. To me, it was delicious, but I didn't dare tell her.

"She likes it." Poppa pointed and smiled at her. "She's doing that bunny nose twitch thing she does when she eats one of those Cadbury Eggs. She loves those."

"You like it, Mama?" I asked. And I wished I hadn't.

"How's it taste?" the waitress asked over my shoulder.

"This is undercooked. Can you get me a new one?" Mama jerked her basket up in the air toward the waitress.

"That's impossible. This has been cooking for a day. It's fresh." The waitress pushed the basket back toward Mama.

"It's undercooked," Mama said a little louder and moved her head left to right as if she were using a horn. "It's slimy."

"It's delicious." I put another forkful in my mouth, trying to drown out Mama.

"It's slimy," Mama said again and pushed back.

"It is not. And you aren't handicapped either." The waitress had a look of disgust on her face and I stuffed mine as full as I could before the next thing happened. "Get out and don't come back."

My eyes followed the length of the woman's arm and down past her finger where she pointed straight for the door. The twirling lights of the tow truck caught my attention. A man stood next to Mama's car.

"What on earth?" Mama jumped up. The coke tipped over and went all over the paper tablecloth.

A few familiar clicks came from the counter where people could mosey up to eat instead of waiting for an open seat at a picnic bench. Behind the big camera lens was a waving feather from a fedora hat. The camera came down slightly; Edna Easterly was staring right at me.

"This ain't good." Poppa's ghost disappeared.

I jumped up after Mama and dropped a couple of twenties on the table before I headed out the door, where she was giving the man from S&S Auto Salvage a mouthful of sass.

"Excuse me." I inserted myself in between him and Mama. "I'm sure we have a misunderstanding here."

"Say, don't I know you?" He snapped his fingers and then shook one at me. "You're that cop that gave us all sorts of trouble."

"I didn't give you trouble. You illegally towed a truck from a crime scene." I reminded him of a murder that'd happened a few months ago. I'd had to get the truck back before they'd made it into a flat piece of steel.

"No." He shook his head. "You gave me trouble and now she's giving me trouble."

The customers in The Little Shack were staring at us from inside, barbeque hanging out of their mouths. Edna was grinning ear to ear, snapping away.

"Just let us go, please," I said in a sweet voice. "We were just trying to grab a bite."

"You're from Cottonwood. That sheriff." The man shuffled to the tow truck and grabbed the heavy chains.

"You're who?" The waitress had stepped out of the diner and stood on the sidewalk, a lit cigarette tucked in the corner of her lip. "Did you say the sheriff?"

"Yep." The chains clanked quite loudly on the ground when he dropped them next to Mama's front tire.

Mama used her shoe to try to push the chain, but it didn't budge.

"Move that chain." Mama demanded. Her key fob pointed at the car, she clicked it several times to unlock the door. "I'm getting in my car."

"You mean to tell me the sheriff is letting this woman use a fake handicap tag?" The cigarette bounced up and down in the woman's mouth. "I'll be darned. I thought I'd seen it all."

"I did no such thing." I started to sweat and got a little nervous. "This is my mama and she had a minor surgery. The doctor gave her the tag."

"I think I read that the sheriff of Cottonwood's mama is competing for that fancy culinary show." The tow truck employee couldn't seem to keep his mouth shut.

"Is that right?" the waitress asked, lowering her eyelids. "Take it away!" the woman instructed him. She tossed the lit cigarette on the ground and used the toe of her shoe to snuff it out before she turned to go back inside.

"I bet she doesn't wash her hands." Mama had no business spitting out more words, but she did.

Poppa was doubled over in laughter. It seemed as though he were thoroughly entertained by his daughter. I ignored him.

"Mama, stay." I put my hand out and tugged off my sweater, exposing my sheriff's uniform. I walked up to the tow truck guy. "Listen, she's old. Can you please just let us go?"

"She's parked illegally." He pointed to the sign that had S&S's number on it. "Violators will be towed."

At least he could read.

"Yeah. But she did get the tag from the doctor." I nodded.

"It's pink. There's no such thing." The man told me something I'd already known, but I was going to ask Dr. Shively about it when I got back to town. She wouldn't give Mama a fake tag.

"You and I both know that things aren't always on the up and up over at S&S." I bit the edge of my lip. I hated to bring politics into it, but Mama left me no choice. "There were a lot of things I forgave and overlooked during that investigation. In fact, I didn't bring charges against you or the company for breaking the crime-scene tape and taking the truck a few months ago and," I hesitated, nodding my head, "the statute of limitations hasn't passed, so I guess I could look into it, have the company shut down until the investigation is over. But then you'd probably have to look for another job." I shrugged.

He gave me a long hard look. He chewed on what I'd said. I could wait him out. I'd learned to be really good at that.

Mama honked the horn and started the car. He glanced up at her and back at me. He bent down and picked up the chains and took a step away from the car.

"Thank you." I curled my lips in a tight grimace and ran around the car and climbed into the passenger side.

"You can get glad in the same britches you got mad in." Mama's jaw was set. "That's all I want to hear about today. I've got to get home and get my ingredients ready for tomorrow."

"Tomorrow?" I asked.

"Yes, silly girl." Mama was giddy and playful. "Frank gets in town today. We have a little get together and tomorrow is the big tasting. Tomorrow is the big day and a fresh pot pie is just what's going to win this for me."

That was Mama. If she didn't want to talk about it, there was no sense in bringing it up. She grabbed her cell phone and jabbed the numbers.

"Hi-do. This here is Viv Lowry and I need an appointment at two please." Mama um-hummed in the phone, agreeing with whoever she'd made an appointment with. I was hoping it was with a shrink because she'd lost her ever-loving mind.

"What was that about?" I asked.

"Kenni, I don't go nosing in your business." She threw the phone in her purse and slammed the gear shift into drive. Who was she trying to fool? Not only was she in my business, she was in everyone's business.

There was no denying the tension in Mama's car on the way back to Cottonwood. I couldn't even bring myself to talk to her for the first fifteen minutes. Not only was I still mad that she'd conned me into going to lunch there, she'd brought me clothes, complained the entire time, and I still had to pay for food I didn't get to finish.

"Did you see Edna Easterly was there?" I felt restless and irritable.

"I hope she got my good side." Mama patted her face.

"Mama." I scolded. "You have got something weird going on in there." I circled her head with my finger. "I think you need to see Dr. Shively about that stuff she stuck in your face."

"I'm fine. I wanted to see my competition. And now I know it's the lack thereof competition. I'm going to win, hands down." She gave a good hard nod.

I didn't say anything the rest of the ride back to the department. The sooner we got back, the sooner I could distance myself from her.

Chapter Six

"There's no resting now," Betty said after I'd gotten back from my awful lunch and flung myself in my office chair. She pointed to the clock. It was only two in the afternoon, but I sure did feel like it was quittin' time.

For a brief moment, I laid my head on the back of my chair with my legs stretched out in front of me and my eyes closed. I was hoping to meditate the lunch away from my mind.

"What now?" I groaned.

"First off, Toots Buford called." She handed me a Post-it with a message from Toots. "She said that there's been some customers parking illegally at the Dixon's Foodtown. Something about pink handicap stickers. She's not the only one who's called. Seems to be a lot of businesses reporting this."

"Pink?" My uh-oh meter went off. There was no way I was going to tell her about Mama's pink one. "Let's give that investigation to Finn."

"Good. Because Ben Harrison called right before you got here and said that Frank Von Lee is in town and coming by the diner in the next half hour. He'd like the sheriff's presence." She looked over the rim of her glasses at me.

Half hour? I glanced up at the clock and that meant he needed me around two p.m.

"Fine," I said with an exhausted sigh, pushing myself up from my chair. "Let's go, Duke."

Within a few seconds, Duke jumped in his usual spot on the

passenger seat of my Wagoneer. I reached over and cranked down his window so he could enjoy the beautiful spring day that popped up. There was nothing like the sight of a fresh crop of the Kentucky bluegrass that blanketed Cottonwood. Today the late afternoon sun was hitting it perfectly and sending the fresh fragrance to my soul. The fresh air didn't hurt either. It seemed to clear my head more than anything.

I took a left out of the alley and stopped at the stoplight to take a left to head down Main Street toward Ben's. The Cottonwood Chronicle box sat on the sidewalk on the corner. From the Jeep, I could see that Edna Easterly had made Frank Von Lee's arrival this week's headline. Mama would have her interview posted next week and being on the front of the Chronicle was better than butter on a biscuit for Mama.

I waved to the people crossing the street. The warmer weather brought them out to peruse our small-town boutiques and antique shops.

There was a big crowd gathered in front of Ben's, no doubt due to Edna's article, where I'm sure she spun more tales than a spinning wheel. Edna was a master at taking a couple of words and making up the biggest story you'd ever heard.

I pulled across the street into a parking spot in front of Ruby Smith's antique shop and parked. Surveying the situation before I got out was probably my best bet to assess how I was going to help Ben with the crowd control. The people stood in front of Ben's and along the sidewalk down to the inn. I remembered the cord of rope I kept in the back of the Jeep, grabbed that, and headed on over. Duke was good at keeping everyone's eyes and hands on him while I made a makeshift red-carpet walkway between the buildings with the rope strung from the trees along the sidewalk for our special guest.

The look on Ben's face told me he was appreciative, though I think he'd spent so much time on the diner he'd forgotten about how to treat Frank Von Lee's arrival.

"Here." Ruby walked over and handed over two Oriental rug runners. "The sheriff's department can borrow them as long as you take them to the cleaners afterward so I can resell them."

"Why, you do have a soft spot," I teased her.

Her brightly painted orange lips snarled as she handed the rugs to me. I stood there and watched her five-foot-nine lanky frame weave through the crowd. You couldn't miss that bright red head of hers. A smile crossed my lips as I unfurled the long rugs and made the perfect runway for our guest.

The crowd had shifted to stand behind the rope. Most of the women in Mama's Sweet Adelines Group—Lulu McClain, Mrs. Kim, Toots Buford, Viola White, Myrna Savage, and Missy Jennings—stood closest to the door. For years they'd bragged on Mama's cooking, but I just figured they were nice compliments with underlying meanings, like our famous saying, bless your heart. It sounded good, but when you shaved back the layers, it was a dagger in the heart and you didn't even know it.

As soon as the doors of The Tattered Cover Books and Inn opened, a collective gasp rose from the crowd. Then there was dead silence as though everyone was holding their breath.

"Good morning." Frank Von Lee took off his top hat and rolled it a few times in front of himself as he took a bow. The man was as bald as a baby's butt, but his handlebar mustache made up for what he didn't have on his head.

He held the top hat against his chest with one hand and a cane in the other. He slowly walked down the runway as though he was at a television premiere and took the time to nod to the people standing behind the rope line. He even stopped for a few photos and gave a few autographs.

He stopped at the diner door and turned around.

"I'm looking forward to sampling the chicken pot pie." His words were very clipped as though there was a period after each

SIX FEET UNDER   41

one of them.

Ben and Mama stood at the door.

"Goodness gracious." Mama's hand lifted to her chest, and she fingered her pearl necklace as she giggled. "Thank you kindly."

"Look at your mama." Ruby Smith had snuck up behind me. "She's so stinkin' happy. I ain't seen her that happy since the day your daddy asked her to marry him."

"Is that right?" I asked and tilted my head to the right to get a better view of Mama doing her southern thing. She'd curled her hand in the crook of Frank Von Lee's elbow and escorted him right on into the diner, her lips never stopping moving once.

Poor man, I thought. He'd know everything there was to know about Mama, me, and Cottonwood by the time he left their little meeting. He'd probably not even get a word in edgewise.

"What's that look for?" Ruby patted my arm. "Honey, don't be goin' and worryin' about your mama. She's in full control."

"That's what I'm worried about." I took a deep breath. The crowd around me had dispersed and Duke sat by my feet.

What they'd come for had been seen. Frank Von Lee and his arrival was now tomorrow's news as the entire town waited for his decision, which wouldn't be coming for a few days. Heck, he wasn't even going to sample Mama's pot pie until tomorrow, and then he'd be going to Clay's Ferry.

The tension was not only in the air, but on Poppa's face as he stood over Mama in the diner as she sat next to Frank Von Lee.

As much as I tried to forget Poppa's face, I couldn't. Seeing him gave me fearful clarity that he was there for something that was about to happen. I just didn't know what.

Chapter Seven

The appearance from Frank Von Lee was just that. He'd only spent about twenty minutes in the diner with Mama and Ben before he excused himself back to his hotel.

After that, I'd made my afternoon rounds in the town and stopped to chat with a few neighbors who were hanging out on their porches. After all, it was getting close to the election. I had to make appearances before I headed on home to change my clothes so I wasn't late to Mama's cooking class at Lulu's Boutique. Finn and I had also made plans to see each other after the class.

Mrs. Brown, my neighbor, was more than happy to take care of Duke while I was gone for the night. I wasn't going to be gone long, but I hated to leave him alone when he could enjoy Mrs. Brown as much as she enjoyed him. Of course, Finn had offered, but I couldn't do that to Mrs. Brown.

Lulu's Boutique, owned by Mama's best friend Lulu McClain, was located on the far end of the north side of town. Lulu had purchased the old run-down clapboard cottage-style house and brought it back to life by giving it a new paint job and refinished hardwood floors. She'd even made the upstairs into an efficiency apartment. The boutique was a little knick-knack shop that sold Kentucky branded items, jewelry, and anything that could have a monogram. We Southerners loved our initials. We even printed them on our cars and bath towels.

There was a line of cars pulled up to the curb outside of

Lulu's. Some I knew and some I didn't. Before I went in, I swiped some lipstick on and grabbed my cell, sticking it in my back pocket. At least Mama would be happy to see I'd attempted some makeup, and that should keep her satisfied.

When I walked by her car, I looked in to see if the handicap tag was dangling from the arm of the rearview, but it wasn't. I made a mental note to ask Mama about that right off.

Lulu's held different classes for the community. I especially loved the craft classes. Generally they were attended by the same old gossipy women I spent one night a week with at our Euchre game. Even though they drove me crazy, they'd showed up tonight for Mama. That's the way it was around Cottonwood. No matter how cotton-pickin' mad someone got at you, they'd be right by your side in your hour of need.

It warmed my heart to see them gathered around Mama with a big smile on her face when I walked in.

"Your mama sure can tell a story." Jolee walked up and handed me a glass of Mama's sweet tea. "She's got everyone in stitches about her meeting with Frank and his hearty appetite."

"Oh brother." I shook my head and wet my whistle. "She's got you calling him Frank too?"

"She makes it sound like they've been friends for years." Jolee laughed. "I'm excited to see exactly what she puts in her pot pie to make it so good. That's why I'm here. I could just smack myself for letting her be on Ben's team."

She was referring to the cook-off. Jolee got to handpick her contestants to go up against Ben's. Trust me when I say that we were all in shock when Mama came out the winner. And now here we were today.

"That barbeque don't have a leg to stand on compared to my pot pie, right, Kenni?" Mama dragged me into her sordid tale.

Lulu, Myrna, Toots, Ruby, and Viola all turned to look at

me, their eyes wide open, waiting on my response.

"I don't know anything about that, Mama." I waved the ladies off. Idle gossip wasn't my glass of sweet tea. "Mama, I wouldn't be going around telling people about our little adventure today," I warned as a bad feeling suddenly washed over me. "It's not very becoming of either of us."

Mama didn't realize that I'd thrown my badge around. Though it wasn't really against the law to remind the tow truck driver how un-businesslike his boss was, it still wasn't the most ethical thing to do. Citizens of Cottonwood held morality in high regard, often forgetting their own mistakes. They'd be quick with their tongues and finger wagging when it came to election time. Though I was currently unopposed, you just never could be too sure.

"Well, we can all take our places." Mama clasped her hands together.

The tables in the back of Lulu's were set up with three workstations each. Mama had already put all the ingredients we needed in little bowls. All except her special ingredient. She said that would be distributed last. Just like Mama to build up the anticipation. She loved that. And loved that it was centered on her.

We all went to our stations. "And lastly," Mama stood up with pride and held the canister with no markings up in the air, "everyone needs to get their tablespoon ready because this is my very special secret."

Mama had made up the cutest four-in-one country blue measuring spoons with her name printed on them. This entire television thing had made her head swell more than usual.

Jolee scooted to the edge of her seat and eagerly grabbed her tablespoon, holding it way out in front of her. Knowing Jolee, she'd figure out the ingredients and try to duplicate them in her own On The Run recipe. That would send Mama off if she did.

"These are cute." Jolee's brows rose to high heaven. "I should probably get something cute like this for the truck," she whispered after Mama gave her the wonky eye.

My phone rang. I gulped and looked up. Mama's glare had turned from Jolee to me. Her moment was stolen by the sound of my phone and it didn't sit well with her.

"Kendrick," Mama shamed me. "That's rude."

"I'm sorry. I've got to take this." I answered when I saw it was the late-night dispatch. Were they calling about Mama's charade from today?

We shared the service with Clay's Ferry dispatch. Neither of our departments needed to be open twenty-four hours a day, so we chipped in and used someone from seven p.m. until eight a.m. to field the calls.

"Sheriff Lowry," I answered.

"Sheriff, there's been an ambulance dispatched to The Tattered Cover Books and Inn. A Dr. Camille Shively called it in," the dispatcher said over the phone. "It's concerning an unresponsive male."

"I'm on my way." The chair clattered to the ground when I stood up in haste. I looked up at Mama, but it wasn't her gaze I met. It was Poppa's. Fear struck the very center of my body. Chills zoomed up my spine like a roller coaster.

"Frank Von Lee is dead." Poppa's words pierced my ears.

"Frank is dead?" The words fell from my mouth.

Chapter Eight

"Wait." Mama ran beside me, the can of her secret ingredient in her hand. "Did you say 'dead' and 'Frank' in the same sentence?"

"Nope. Didn't say a word." I ran faster to my Wagoneer. The less Mama knew, the better off I was.

"Kendrick Lowry. You said Frank is dead. I might be old, but I'm not hard-of-hearing old." Mama stood at the door of the Wagoneer.

"Gotta go, Mama." I grabbed the old beacon siren from underneath my seat and licked the suction cup, sticking it to the roof of the Jeep. I slid my finger down the side and caught the switch for the siren.

I threw the Jeep in gear, did a U-turn, and put the pedal to the metal. Immediately I dialed Finn and left no room for chitchat. Nothing but, "Meet me at the inn. Frank Von Lee is dead," then I hung up. Within minutes, I was standing with my sheriff's bag tight in my grip in Frank Von Lee's room, where Camille Shively looked a bit disheveled and Poppa was standing next to her over Frank's body, surrounded by EMTs. Finn arrived soon after.

"I've been doing CPR, but he's not coming back." Camille gasped for breath before she went back down to give Frank more CPR while the EMTs were doing chest compressions. "You keep doing compressions and I'll keep breathing."

Her long black hair that was normally neatly parted to the side and hung down to her collarbones in a flawless cascade was pulled back in a messy ponytail. Something she'd obviously done to get it out of the way. She wasn't going to step back and let the EMTs do their job.

"Doctor." One of the EMTs stopped doing the compressions and patted the other to stop too. "Ma'am, I don't think we're going to bring him back."

"Nope. Nope. They aren't." Poppa put his hands in his pants pockets. "This whole situations smells bad enough to knock a dog off a gut wagon."

That was bad, and he didn't mean the smell in the room.

"He's dead. I think you need to call it." I tapped Camille on the shoulder. "Camille." I tapped harder.

"Not on my dime, Kenni," she said through gritted teeth. By the crack in her voice, I knew that she knew he was gone. She glanced at the EMTs. Her pale skin was even whiter. The whites of her eyes were tinted red. "What are you doing? Don't stop."

They stood up, but she was relentless for about three more minutes, going back and forth between doing the compressions and the breathing herself. Finally, she sat back on her heels and put her head in her hands, sobbing.

"Oh, no." A gasp came from the door of the room Frank Von Lee had rented. "Well, this just butters my biscuit."

"Mama." I looked at Finn. "Please take her out of here and call Max Bogus for me."

Finn rushed over and grabbed Mama. Mama didn't like it one bit.

Max Bogus had a dual job as our county coroner and the undertaker of Cottonwood's only funeral home. He'd come and make an initial report before taking the body to do a final autopsy.

"Kenni."

I looked at Poppa when he said my name. He was pointing to the small brown desk that sat in front of the window.

I walked over to the desk and let Camille collect herself.

"This is why you're here," I muttered.

"That pot pie looks familiar." Poppa pointed to the plate. Next to it was an empty glass. "If I'm not mistaken, that's a plate from Ben's Diner."

"Sheriff," one of the EMTs called. "Is there anything else you need us for?"

I turned around, shaking my head.

"No. Thank you for all you've done. I got it from here." I turned back to the window and peeled the curtain away from the glass. "My deputy called the coroner so he should be here any minute."

"We'll get our report to you," the EMT said before they gathered their equipment and left.

The window looked out over Main Street and I could see news had spread fast. There was already a crowd lined up around the ambulance and the Jeep.

"This is the first patient I've ever lost." Camille's voice broke the silence and the stillness that death always seemed to bring.

"And to be a famous man to boot." Poppa shrugged. "This doesn't look good." He ghosted himself over to Frank's body. "There's a bit of the pot pie stuck on the front of his shirt."

"I'm sorry, Camille." I didn't have the words to comfort her. Dealing with the emotions following death was never easy for me. Though I wanted to cry out and beg that this hadn't happened again on my watch, as sheriff, I had to hide those emotions and do my job. "I am going to need a statement from you."

I placed my bag on the floor and took out the small tape recorder. I felt it was best to have a general conversation with her while I made her more at ease by taking photos of the crime scene after putting the yellow crime-scene tape along the door. I pressed record and got to work.

"I got a phone call on the emergency line. The operator said there was a call from room number three. He'd not given his name to the operator. They said he was slurring his words." Her eyes slid over to look at Frank. She fidgeted.

"Try not to touch anything." I knew it was a strong statement.

"You think this is a murder scene?" She jerked her hand off his body. Frank was getting bluer by the minute.

"I haven't ruled anything out. Do you have any suspicion on a cause of death?" I asked.

"Well, I came in and he was on the bed. Alive." Her words faded into the space around us.

"Kenni, this doesn't look good for your mama. My daughter." There was a sudden fear in Poppa's voice I'd yet to hear since he'd come back as a ghost. "I'm telling you there is something wrong with this pot pie."

What was Frank doing with some of Mama's pot pie? Where'd he get it from? Mama had mentioned that she'd planned on making the pot pie Frank was going to be critiquing in the morning. "Let it sit for a spell. Thickens up the liquid." Mama claimed that was part of her special recipe.

I snapped a few photos of the pot pie as Camille continued to talk into the tape recorder.

"He was alive. Talking. I asked him where he felt sick. He said that he'd been working and felt an onset of nausea. He went to lay down for a bit because of some pain in his stomach. He called 911 when the abdominal pain didn't go away after an hour." She continued to gnaw on the edge of her lip.

I put on a pair of gloves from my bag and used my finger to move around the papers on the desk next to the plate. When I saw one had Mama's name on it, I picked it up.

"He started to sweat and got really confused." Camille's

voice was in the background. I wasn't really listening, which was awful to admit, but Frank's written words had caught my attention.

Mrs. Vivian Lowry, though tall in the charming southern way, fell short in my expectations of the chicken pot pie that's staked her claim to fame in her small town of Cottonwood. The chicken was tough. For a pot pie, the number one rule is to pre-cook the chicken barely pale so the baking process will tenderize it to a juicy goodness. Mrs. Lowry claims the crust is where her secret ingredient is hidden away. All I know that's hidden is the big secret she's keeping from patrons of Ben's Diner: using a readymade flour mix from a box. There was nothing special about it. The only part of the pot pie that was even remotely tasty was the larger-than-normal sized vegetables used.

"I continued to tell him who I was and where he was. He got confused and agitated." Camille's voice grew stronger and louder. "That's when he stood up, grabbed his chest, and fell to the ground." She huffed a few times through her nose. "I think I'm going to be sick." She stumbled to the bathroom and let go of anything she'd had in her stomach.

I folded the paper in half and stuck it in my pocket.

"You know it too." Poppa appeared. "Get rid of the evidence."

"There is nothing here that says Mama did him in." I ran my hand down the front pocket of my pants where I'd put the note.

"Kenni, if your mama walked in here and saw that review he was working on, she'd have lost her marbles." Poppa paced back and forth, his hands clasped behind his back. "She's been driving herself nuts since she got word he was coming. I've been with her. She's not slept. She did that thing to her face."

Poppa was right. Mama had been acting out of the ordinary, beyond her usual crazy antics.

"I shouldn't've ignored her behavior like I did." The thought of it made me want to grab the pot pie and throw it in my bag. I reached my hand out to take it.

"Go on. If she did it, there'll be more evidence. This buys us time to think." For the first time, Poppa made me question his honesty in his time as sheriff. But family deserved loyalty.

"I can keep the review and shred it. I can flush the pot pie or throw it in my bag. No one will immediately know he was eating it. Though Max will find it in his belly." I put my fingers on the rim of the plate.

"And it will buy us time," Poppa repeated.

"It'll buy us time to get her a lawyer. A real lawyer, not Wally Lamb." The thought that this town that Mama loved so much was going to turn their backs on her broke me to my core.

"Kenni." Finn rushed into the room.

I jerked my hand away from the pot pie. What on earth had gotten into me? I knew. Poppa had gotten to me.

"Dagnabit!" Poppa ghosted himself away.

"What happened?" He was quickly followed in by Max Bogus. Camille walked out of the bathroom with a washcloth on her head. Finn greeted her with a nod.

My moral compass took over and I slipped the review out of my pocket and underneath the plate. What was I thinking? I wasn't. I sucked in a deep breath, and the smell of death hung in my nostrils.

"Please, can we do this later?" Camille asked. "I'm not feeling well and there's really no more I can do about this situation."

"Kenni, do you care if Dr. Shively leaves?" Finn wasn't going to let her go without my consent since he didn't know what'd taken place before he'd gotten here.

"Sure, I'm fine with it. Please come by the station tomorrow to give a formal statement." I offered a smile. "Camille..."

Though we both grew up in Cottonwood, we weren't what I considered good friends, but I cared about her. "I'm really sorry you had to go through this. You did all you could do to help him."

She pursed her lips as if she were holding back tears and nodded a couple of times before she rushed out of the hotel room.

Chapter Nine

"Thoughts?" I asked Max Bogus after he'd stepped back out of the room into the hallway.

"I won't know anything for sure until I do an autopsy, but from the sound of Camille's statement, he probably had a heart attack. Given his lifestyle of eating all sorts of fatty foods, not to mention not being in the best shape, it's all the classic signs." Max took a deep inhale.

"Kenni, can I see you?" Finn stuck his head out of the door. His eyes bore into me.

"Kenni! Kenni!" Katy Lee Hart trilled from down the end of the hallway.

"What on earth is she doing here?" I asked and gave Finn the hold-on-a-second gesture.

I met Katy Lee halfway down the hall. How did she do it? I wondered how day in and day out Katy Lee looked fresh as a daisy. For a thicker gal, she walked with more grace and dignity than any thin girl I ever saw. Her silk shirt dress had the sweetest beautiful botanicals with a simple sweet lace collar. She even had a piece of grosgrain ribbon neatly tied as a waist-defining accent. Her cowboy boots made it even cuter.

"Kenni." Katy Lee's eyes dipped in sadness. "I just heard what happened. This is awful."

"Yeah. Say, what are you doing here?" I asked, trying to sound nonchalant.

"Kenni?" Her face contorted. "Frank Von Lee is dead and

you want to know why I'm here?"

"You know I can't say anything, so I want to hear something good." I shrugged. "Like what's going on with you?"

"You can't tell me the tiniest bit?" She lifted her fingers an inch apart in front of our faces. "Fine." She seemed to be satisfied at my "no" face. "I've got the annual Shabby Trends summer fashion show today."

Shabby Trends was a clothing line that Katy Lee sold out of her house, kinda like Tupperware, only clothing. It wasn't just any clothing line. They were fancy duds that I rarely wore, but I supported my friend and attended all her parties.

"I sent you an invitation and you did RSVP." Her lips twitched to the side and her eyes glanced past my shoulder toward the crime scene. "I guess you have a valid excuse, though I do have the cutest dress that would go great with your hair color." There was always a piece that Katy picked out for me. Usually the most expensive. "I've held it back for you."

"Thank you. Do you have a full house?" I asked. I'd actually forgotten about the fashion show.

"Yes. And your mama was here earlier." A broad smile crossed her face. "I'm going to pick out some pieces for you and let her buy them. She said she'd pick them up from me at the agency. Now that you have a boyfriend, you need to have some new clothes for dates." She winked.

Katy Lee's family owned Hart Insurance Agency in the strip mall. She was an insurance agent during the day and Shabby Trends consultant the rest of the time.

"Did you send Mama an invitation?" I found it particularly odd she'd invite Mama since Shabby Trends was more of a clothing line for the ages between twenty and fifty and she'd never invited her before. Though Mama insisted she felt my age, she certainly wouldn't dress in Shabby Trends clothing.

"Nope. I figured she knew about it because of you." Katy

Lee shook her head. "She was coming down out of the stairway door while I was coming down the hall to set up the fashion show. We practically ran into each other. Well, she did run into me, as if she were in a rush." She rolled her eyes. "They put us in that old library room. I wish there was another room we could use, but it's the biggest when you move all those old dreary tables out of the way."

"She was coming out of the stairway?" I asked.

Mama never took the stairs. She said they made her sweat, and Mama didn't like the slightest bit of sweating.

"Yes. She seemed upset, so I figured I'd tell her you liked this one particular shirt and she must see it. Anything having to do with you takes her mind off whatever upsets her."

"Do you remember the time?" I asked.

"It was around supper time because my stomach was growling when Nanette served the guests a meatloaf to die for." Katy Lee smacked her lips together, referring to the hotel's owner and manager. "Speaking of food, do you know how your mama's meeting with Frank went?"

"A meeting?" I asked urgently.

"Kenni Lowry, are you okay?" She drew back, staring before she narrowed her eyes and slightly shifted her head to the side, looking at me all side-goggling.

"I'm fine, but Mama didn't have her meeting until tomorrow." My head was all foggy. I felt like I was having an out-of-body experience. Mama had motive and opportunity to kill Frank Von Lee.

"Hmm." Katy Lee pressed her lips together. "I thought I overheard her ask Nanette what room number Frank had." She gave a slight shrug. "Oh well. I probably heard wrong and just assumed they were getting together."

"They did have the initial meeting at Ben's in the early afternoon. Is that what you mean?" I asked.

"No. She was here earlier, but I couldn't say anything to her then because I was packing in all my clothes. But after she ran into me, that's when I talked her into buying you some new clothes," Katy said.

"What time was it that you got here?" I didn't want it to seem so obvious that I was trying to get a timeline for Mama's whereabouts.

Her nose curled and her lip twitched as though she were searching for the time up in her head. "Sometime around four-ish. I think." She waved her hand at me. "You know me. I was so focused on getting set up that I didn't pay much attention to it."

"There you are. People are waiting to fill orders before you close up." Whitney Hart had stopped at the top of the steps that lead up to the rooms. Her hair was pulled back in a low ponytail, her gold earrings dangling. She wore a denim shirt dress with a big braided belt around the waist and a pair of sandals with gold straps. "Kenni, how are you? I heard about that fancy food critic. Shame."

"Hi, Mrs. Hart." I offered a sympathetic smile. The last time I'd directly talked to her was when I had to tell her about Rowdy, her son. He was murdered a while back and I knew this was bringing back some hurtful memories of that time.

"It's a shame." I nodded.

"If it was a heart attack, it's the way to go. Sudden." She placed a hand on Katy Lee. "Come on, your daddy's at home waiting on me."

"Bye, Katy Lee, Mrs. Hart." I waved to them.

The walk back to the room seemed long as I thought of Mama coming to the inn with her pot pie—which seemed like a bribe. If she did ask Nanette his room number and go up there, that put Mama at the scene. Not to mention a good motive to kill him was in the written words he'd put on that piece of paper. Not good for Mama if Frank Von Lee was murdered.

Chapter Ten

It took a few snooze buttons, a hot shower, and a couple cups of coffee to get me going the next morning. The investigation into Frank's death had gone late into the night with very little evidence gathered to make it seem like a murder. Finn hadn't called or stopped by. Max Bogus hadn't called. And Poppa wasn't around.

I wasn't sure whether to be happy or worried. Either way, it was a new day and I still had a job to do and a possible murder to solve. The Cottonwood Chronicle was delivered every morning around five a.m. and I couldn't help but think when I saw Mama sitting proudly next to her freshly baked pot pie from her interview at the diner she'd be proud as a peach this morning even though her dreams of being on the television show were dashed.

A little bit of recognition in the Chronicle would make her happy. Or at least temper her mood about the death of Frank Von Lee and her lost chance.

"Duke." I stood with my back up against the counter of my kitchen, my legs crossed at the ankles, a cup of coffee in one hand and the paper in the other.

Duke had just gobbled up the last bits of his kibble and his droopy eyes looked up at me.

"You ready to go bye-bye?" It was the trigger word he knew meant get in the Jeep and get out of here.

His growl and loud bark followed by the prance to the door

signaled he was ready to go. I grabbed my cell off the counter along with my sheriff's bag, took the keys from the hook, and headed out the back door.

I'm not going to lie. I looked down the street toward Finn's house to see if he was home. When I didn't see his Dodge Charger, I wondered where he'd gone so early. Come to think of it, I didn't see his car there when I let Duke out before bed, which was around midnight. Maybe he had a lead on the handicap sticker investigation and was checking into those.

"You still have a hankerin' for that boy." Poppa appeared in the passenger seat of the Jeep. Duke jumped to the back.

I pulled the Jeep to a complete stop at the stop sign at the end of the street.

"What are you doing here? Not that I'm not happy to see you, but I figured since I'd not seen you since the inn that you were gone." I was searching for answers that my gut told me I feared most. "I'm guessing Frank's death wasn't accidental."

"You'd be right." Poppa stared at the window. "I guess you better head on over to your mama and daddy's to check on her."

"Is that a mere suggestion or are you telling me to go?" There were two sides to Poppa, his loving family side and his sheriff's side. His voice told me this was his sheriff's side.

"I think you know what's going to come down the line" were Poppa's last words before he ghosted away.

In frustration, I smacked the wheel with the palm of my hand. What good was having a ghost deputy if there were more questions than answers?

I jerked the wheel to the right and headed in the opposite direction of the department, downtown toward my family home. Normally I'd have called Max Bogus by now to see what the initial autopsy had said and what the plans were for Frank's body, but I couldn't bring myself to find out the answers too quickly considering that I already feared the worst.

My childhood home was a modest three-bedroom brick ranch. There was a long covered porch on the front and a nice patio on the back. If you came in through the left side of the house through the garage door, it led into a laundry room with a full bath, traveling into a kitchen nook, passing through the kitchen and into the family room that led to a hall with the three bedrooms and a bath at the end. In the front of the house, through the front door was a small entryway that spilled into the hallway, or you could go left into the living room.

The living room was the fancy room with the expensive furniture that Mama had bought down at Goodlett's Furniture. You couldn't sit in there unless it was Christmas. That's where we opened presents. Mama insisted on having the furniture in the Christmas photos, never mind that my hair was stuck up all over the place and the wrapping paper was strewn all over the floor.

It was also the room where she'd hold court with her Sweet Adelines and whatever other social gatherings she'd have.

I walked up to the front door and knocked. Dad opened the door. I looked up at him. He still towered over me, and for his age, he remained in good physical shape. His brown eyes were tired and sagged a little more than usual. His brown hair was starting to get a little grey in it, but if I dared to say anything, Mama would have him down at Tiny Tina's for a color. I wasn't going to put him through that again.

"You don't want to come in here." He rolled his eyes. "Your mama acts like it's a funeral in here."

Duke shoved his nose in the door and pushed his ninety-pound body into the house.

"He does." I laughed and stepped into the foyer. "What's going on with Mama?"

The corners of Dad's eyes drooped. "She's been up all night. She came home and told me about Frank."

"What did she do all night?" I asked.

"The funny thing is that she did nothing." Dad shrugged. "I waited to see if I needed to call Dr. Shively to get your mama some of them relaxing pills, but she simply grabbed her robe and went to the bathroom where she took a long bath and read one of her romance books while she soaked."

"She didn't say a word?" I thought that was strange.

"Not a single peep." Dad shook his head.

"Stayed up and read all night. You and I both know that ain't like your mama. It all started yesterday afternoon after she said she was taking you to a mother-daughter lunch. What happened on that lunch?" Daddy had a curious look on his face.

"She didn't have any intentions of having any daughter time." I cocked a brow. "She took me to the barbecue restaurant in Clay's Ferry that was going to be her competition."

Dad's face held a blank stare before he closed his eyes for a brief moment.

"That explains the weird cooking talk she did after she came home." He suctioned his tongue on the front of his teeth like he always did when he was thinking.

"What do you mean?" I asked. I had a nigglin' that every single moment of Mama's whereabouts needed to be accounted for.

"She came in, muttered something about needing some creamer for a new recipe, and took off again. She seemed really distant." He shrugged.

"Did she do anything different to the pot pie she'd been making?" I'd questioned the comment he made about creamer because I knew Mama used milk.

"Not a word. She just left, and I didn't see her again until she came in last night when she told me about Frank." He smacked his lips together when we heard movement coming down the hall.

"Kenni." Mama walked into the foyer with a big pair of black sunglasses covering her eyes. "What are you doing here?"

Dad walked away, but not without running a loving hand down Mama's arm.

"Mama." I reached out my arms. She was in a time of need. I bet she'd been crying all night from the news of Frank Von Lee and Dad didn't even notice. "I'm so sorry."

"Are you okay?" I ran a hand down her arm. In the background I could hear Daddy and Duke in the kitchen eating God knows what.

"I'll be fine." Mama brought the back of her finger up to her nose and gave a little sniffle.

"I'd love a cup of coffee," I suggested, since Mama wasn't about to offer me nothing.

"Not today." She sighed a little weepily and turned back around.

"Well, I'm having a cup of coffee." I pushed past her. She jerked around, her glasses falling to the ground. "Mama!" I gasped and drew my hand up to my mouth when I saw her big black and blue eye. "What on earth happened?"

"It's nothing. Act as though you never saw it and you must not speak a word of it," she whispered and scurried off toward her bedroom.

"Daddy. Daddy," I called on my way to the kitchen. I pointed behind me toward the hall. "What in the hell happened to Mom's eye? Did she fall?" I wondered if she'd slipped getting out of the tub.

"I don't know. She wouldn't tell me." He threw a piece of his toast to Duke, who gladly snapped it up.

"She's got a black eye." My jaw dropped. "Dad." I gulped and rushed over to the kitchen table, sitting down next to him. "What happened?"

Dad stood up. "You need to ask her. I think she's lost her

cotton-pickin' mind over this television show and now that the chef is dead, she's really gone bonkers. She won't tell me how she got the black eye."

"Dad, how did she get the black eye?" I demanded. "How do you not know? You live with her."

"I told you to ask her. She tells me not to worry about it." He gave me a kiss on the forehead and put his dish in the dishwasher.

My mind swirled back to Frank's written review. I'd seen Mama strike someone with her words and they could do damage, but I'd never seen her get into a physical altercation. Had she with Frank? There were two things that were strange to me. One, Poppa was here and he only came when there was a murder. Two, Mama was at the Inn around the time of the murder and now she has a black eye. Poppa being here told me Frank was murdered. But what did Mama know, if anything, about it?

"Kenni!" Betty's voice pierced my ear through my walkie-talkie and brought me out of my head. "Get over to Max Bogus's right away. It's urgent. He's got some results."

"Results?" Mama poked her head in the room. "Did she say Max Bogus?"

"On my way, Betty." I grabbed Duke by the collar and dragged both of us out of the house as Mama continued to nip at my heels. "Mama," I turned around after I'd gotten Duke in the car, "I don't know what Max wants. I'll let everyone know when I find out."

Mama gnawed on the edge of her lip as I left her standing in her driveway when I pulled out.

"I don't like this one bit, Kenni-bug." Poppa ghosted himself next to Duke, holding on to the handle of the Wagoneer as we drove to Max's place with the siren blaring and lights flashing.

"Don't put the cart before the horse. Maybe Max is going to tell us that Frank had a heart attack and all this worry is for nothing." If ever there needed to be a bright side to anything, it was now.

In no time, I parked the Jeep in front of Cottonwood Funeral Home, the only funeral home in our town. The county morgue was in the basement. Like most businesses, the funeral home was in an old Victorian house that'd been remodeled. The old wood floors and dark crown molding were preserved but still gave me the creeps.

A few minutes later, I found Max standing over Frank Von Lee's body in the morgue with his lab coat on, gloves and many gadgets scattered around the small metal table next to him. Frank was hooked up to the lines that were draining him of his blood.

"I came as quick as I could." Out of breath, I stood at the door and looked at the dead body. No matter how many dead bodies I'd seen, it didn't get any easier. I felt a little queasy.

"You aren't going to like what I have to say." When Max looked up, I could see the look in his eyes I'd only been seeing in the last couple of years.

"Frank Von Lee didn't die of a heart attack?" I asked hesitantly.

"He did. But with the help of a little-known poison called Compound 1080. Also known as sodium fluoroacetate. It was found in the preliminary test I ran last night with a blood panel. I also pulled some samples of the food in his stomach and bowels to see if I can pinpoint to source the 1080 was disguised in because the poison has no taste once cooked." Max's eyes did a slow glide from Frank's body to me. "He was murdered."

Chapter Eleven

"I'm not so stupid." Poppa jabbed his head with his fingertip. "Things are addin' up. And it don't look good for your mama."

"Shhh." I closed my eyes and waved my hand in the air, shaking my head. "Stop!"

"But I thought you'd want to know all the facts as I got them, like we always do." Max's voice was tight as he spoke.

I opened my eyes.

"No. No. Not you," I said to Max and looked around for Poppa. He wasn't there. Finally, my lungs fully filled and some oxygen made it into my brain, clearing away the fog. "My head is throbbing. I was doing that whole talking-to-myself thing that's all the rage. Like how women say something to themselves in the mirror to help them feel empowered."

Max looked at me like I had lost my marbles. I wanted to tell him that he was right. I had lost every bit of sense I'd possessed, because it was right about now that I wished I'd stolen that review and the food. But it was not time to fuss over it now. Now was the time to get the evidence and get Mama off my list of suspects.

"Mama," I mouthed when I realized she'd just become my number one suspect.

"What?" Max asked. "Are you okay?"

"I'm fine. Do you have a report?" I asked, trying to forget all the evidence against Mama and be a lot more objective.

"Yep. It's on the counter." He nodded.

Incomplete thoughts swirled in my head, and my legs felt spongy. Swaying a bit, I leaned up against the counter.

"That's your copy," he said, making me grateful for his words.

"I'm going to head back to the office and go over this. I'll give you a call." I took a deep breath to get enough strength to push myself off the counter and headed out of the morgue.

Later I knew I was going to have to explain my strange actions to Max, but first I had to get to Finn.

When I got back to the Jeep, Duke was busy letting everyone who passed pat his head that was stuck out of the window.

"Finn, where are you?" I asked as soon as he answered his phone.

"I'm on my way back to the office. Toots called to tell me someone with the fake handicap tag was in Dixon's. But by the time I got there, they'd left." He sounded a little frustrated. "Are people that lazy they'd buy fake handicap tags?"

"Did you check with the county clerk's office to make sure there wasn't a special breast cancer drive where they turned the tags pink?" It was a good thought.

"I did. Doolittle Bowman said no," he said. "What about you? Anything back on Frank Von Lee?"

"I was just at Max's and his initial autopsy shows Frank Von Lee was poisoned by a compound called 1080." Gripping the wheel with both hands, I decided to tell him what I was thinking. "And without really digging too deep into suspects, I'm fearing Mama is number one."

"What?" He exaggerated the "wh" out of disbelief.

I drove down the alley and pulled in behind Finn's Charger. I could see his silhouette from the back window.

"I just pulled up behind you." I clicked off the phone. Duke took a leap over me and out the window before I could even open the door.

Finn got out of the car and met me. "What on earth is going on?" There was a tenderness in his expression that in an odd way made me feel somewhat better.

I looked both ways down the alley. "Let's go inside."

Betty was aflutter when we walked in.

"The phone hasn't stopped ringing since the news about Frank Von Lee's death." She jabbed a button and said, "Sheriff's department. Calm down. Calm down. There's not a serial killer on the loose. Yes, Mayor." Betty snapped her fingers at me. "She's right here, Mayor."

I walked over to my desk and threw the file from Max on top. I slumped down in my chair.

"Mayor, line two," Betty said before she answered the next call. Finn also jumped on the phones. "He said that Frank was murdered. Is that true?"

I help up a finger for her to hold on.

"Hello, Chance." I tried to sound as upbeat as I could. "I'm sorry. I just got the report from Max and I haven't read it yet, but..." The mayor informed me that Max was doing his job, keeping him abreast of the situation. "Yes, sir. I'm more than happy to go over the report and come see you. I really don't think there's a need for a council meeting."

"I'm worried that if the rumors are true and your mother is a suspect, you won't be able to investigate without having a biased opinion. Not that I think Viv did it, but it's not ethical." He was right, but I wasn't about to tell him that.

"What rumors?" I asked.

"According to Max's report, he was poisoned. According to your report, there was a chicken pot pie on his desk and it had some bites taken out of it. According to Max's report, there was chicken pot pie in his stomach," Chance said. "It don't take no genius to figure out that Frank was only in town because of your mama's chicken pot pie that she was making for him."

"Kenni, your mama is on line three." Finn put three fingers in the air.

"Mayor, I'll give you a call soon. I've got a call about the case that I need to take," I said.

I clicked the receiver before he could protest and hit the blinking button on line three. I had to give myself some thinking room on what he'd said. I knew he was going to ask me to step down from the case. It was something that anyone would question. But now that the shoe was on my foot, there was no way I wanted to back off the case.

"Mama. What's going on?" I asked.

"There's a matinee at Luke Jones's at two this afternoon. Meet me there. I've got something to tell you about Frank Von Lee." She hung up.

I held the phone up to my ear and let out a few laughs, uh-huhs, and okays pretending it was a no big deal conversation with her.

"Okay. Love you too, Mama." I faked a giggle and hung up.

"What did she do?" Finn asked after he sat in one of the chairs in front of my desk.

"Who?" I asked.

Betty was running around the room doing odds and ends to make it appear as if she wasn't listening, but I could clearly see her eyes snapping in my direction to see what I was doing.

"Your mama." His brow rose.

"Nothing. Why?" I kept it short and sweet. I should've told him that Mama had something to tell me, but I just couldn't. It was my mama.

"Well, first off, you said a few minutes ago that she's our number one suspect and secondly," he exhaled, "you just told her you loved her with a giggle. You never do that."

"Listen." I could feel the frustration that Mama was clearly a suspect ripple deep in my gut. Through gritted teeth, I said, "You and I both know that was pot pie. Plus the note."

"What about it?" he asked.

"Did you read it?" I asked.

"No. I just put it in the evidence bag in case it came back as a homicide." A curious look crossed his face. "What did it say?"

"Go read it while I catch up on the report," I suggested and opened the file.

A few more fielded calls later, a quick review of Max's initial report—poisoning through the food—and Finn was back over to my desk.

"Kenni," his voice was resigned, "this isn't good."

"What's not good is that Katy Lee Hart can place Mom at the inn around Frank's time of death." I pushed the file across my desk to Finn.

He picked it up and opened it.

"What did she say?" He asked.

"Katy Lee owns that Shabby Trends. Every season she has a fashion show for the women in the community and it's hosted at the hotel. She said that Mama was upset and practically ran into her after Mama had come from the stairwell. What doesn't make sense is why he had the pot pie when he wasn't supposed to have it until the next day," I said.

Finn jumped up and started to write down things on the white board. Unfortunately, he wrote down Mama's name right in the suspect number one block.

He loved that board. It was the first thing he installed after he'd been sworn in as my new deputy. He claims it helped him see holes along with alibis and theories for cases.

"And remember how she took you to lunch, but really went to check out the competition." He reminded me of the gawd-awful event, making it worse by writing it down.

"Okay. Let's do a timeline." I pushed myself back from the

desk and got up. I took one of the dry-erase markers and wrote down yesterday's date with a big long line. "We can check dispatch, but we can start here when I went to eat with mama in Clay's Ferry and then the diner to make the red carpet entrance."

"Very good." He nodded.

"Mama was there. She was happy and she talked to Frank. It was around two p.m." I wrote down the time. Underneath the timeline, Finn wrote down Mama's actions. I specifically remember looking up at the clock when Betty had told me not to get too comfortable because Ben had called and wanted me to be at the diner upon Frank's arrival.

"What time did she pick you up to go to Clay's Ferry?" He gnawed on the cap of the pen.

"Around eleven a.m." I watched as he wrote the activities and time.

"What time was the cooking class?" He asked.

"Seven," I said matter-of-factly. "But it's the space in between six and seven p.m. that we need to have her accounted for."

"Why's that?" He asked. "Just so we have clarification and get on the right page here."

"Because Max said that once the poison is in your system, you have about thirty minutes at the most until you start having symptoms." I walked over to the desk and pulled the file closer to me, flipping through to Camille's statement. "Camille states here that he was fine when she first got there, but then became confused, angry, upset, and in pain. That was around six forty-five."

"The records also show that the dispatch call came in around 6:50 and they got in touch with you around seven. Right?" he asked.

"Yes." There was a hesitation in my voice because I was

trying to figure out how mama could be put at the scene of the crime with all the driving time she'd been doing.

"You're hesitating." Finn had learned to read me so well.

"If Mama poisoned the pot pie, why? What would've been her motive at that point?" I asked.

"I see where you're going with this." He nodded. "If the pot pie was poisoned and given to him to eat, that would've been premeditated and she'd had to have been mad about something with him before he'd even tasted her pot pie."

"And that's not Mama," I said.

"So it's more important than ever that we fill in this time." He made an arrow on the timeline between two p.m. after Mama had dropped me off and six p.m. when mama was last seen at the Tattered Cover Books and Inn. "If she didn't talk or see Frank between these times and their only meeting was with Ben at the diner around two, then she'd really have no motive to kill him. Especially since he wasn't going to try her pot pie until tomorrow."

"Right. All was good in Mama's world. She was very confident that she was going to beat out the barbeque joint in Clay's Ferry after we left." Something else popped into my head. "She made a phone call."

"To who?" Finn asked.

"I'm not sure. She didn't want to tell me. If she won't tell me, I'll pull her phone records." I gnawed on the thought for a minute.

I looked up at the whiteboard. There certainly wasn't enough evidence to arrest Mama or even point the finger at her. In big letters I wrote "Suspect Number Two" with a question mark underneath.

"It looks like we have more digging to do." Finn stood back and tilted his head to the right and left as if the killer's name was going to magically appear. "Did you see or talk to her between the time you left the diner and the time you saw her at the cooking class?"

"Yes, at the diner when Frank got into town. But my dad said that she came home and muttered something about a new recipe. Got a change of clothes and left. After she'd gotten home from the diner, she was working on some different recipes. Not pot pie."

"The next sighting of Viv was by Katy Lee, around dinner time." Finn wrote down the time, place, and people who saw Mama. "Katy said it was around the time Nanette was about to serve supper. She serves around six o'clock, but by the time she made it around to the people who ordered room service and those eating in the restaurant, the time could vary. According to Max, the poison had to be ingested about thirty minutes before the symptoms. The poison doesn't have a taste. Which puts it around six to six fifteen-ish, because Camille got the call around six-thirty." He wrote his words on the board.

"Katy Lee also said that she thought she'd overheard Mama ask Nanette what room Frank Von Lee was in."

I wrote Nanette's name on the board with an arrow under it and wrote "owner of the Tattered Cover Books and Inn" along with the six o'clock supper time.

Both of us sat there in silence looking at the board, our heads shifting side to side as if seeing it from a different angle would give a different perspective.

"I went to see Mama this morning. She's got a black eye." Every word out of my mouth made it worse and worse for her. "You and I both know that it takes about twelve hours for bruises to show up."

"The plate of chicken pot pie and the review were in his room." Finn paced back and forth. "Your mama was nervous about the competition, gave Frank the pot pie, went back to see if he liked it and saw the note. She got angry and they got into a scuffle."

Here we were, back to trying to make Mama the suspect. Or even just make sense of why she'd kill him.

"That wouldn't make sense." My eyes narrowed as my mind worked overtime trying to take Mama out of the scene of the crime. "If the pot pie was laced with the poison, mama wouldn't've gone back to see if he liked it. I know mama. She might've lost her mind once she saw the review he'd written. She didn't have motive to put poison in the pot pie."

There were so many unanswered questions that only Mama could answer.

Poppa appeared with a little jig in his step. "I went by your mama's house and looked around for some sodium fluoroacetate."

"What do we know about sodium fluoroacetate?" I asked and walked over to grab the file.

"According to Max's report, the sodium fluoroacetate doesn't have a taste when put into food." Finn made a good point.

"Symptoms are," I read Max's writing to Finn as he wrote them down, "nausea, vomiting, and abdominal pain within one hour of ingestion. Victim had classic signs of sweating and reported to be confused and agitated before the heart attack. All of this goes with Camille's recollection."

Everything was there. What were we missing?

"Heart attack?" Finn asked.

"Yeah." My brows drew together. "I guess I've been so focused on how the poison got into Frank's system that I forgot to tell you that he actually died of a heart attack brought on by the sodium fluoroacetate." I hesitated, but I knew I had to tell Finn everything. "When Mama just called, she told me to meet her at the matinee. She had some information to share about Frank."

"Are you going to try to get her to clarify some things?" Finn watched me intently. My heart sank and it must've shown on my face. "She needs to help herself."

"This afternoon I'm going to go question her. I'll bring her in if I feel like she did it." Only that would mean that she had premediated Frank's murder, and I knew my mama. She didn't like to get her hands dirty with dirt, much less a murder. "In the meantime, I'm going to head to the diner and question Ben about the meeting they had yesterday when Frank got to town. Maybe he can tell me something about the conversation or why Mama would take Frank the pot pie early." I grabbed the file and stuck it in my police bag. "If she did take him the pot pie."

Both of us stopped talking when Duke jumped up and ran to the door.

"Sorry." Riley Titan, the contractor, stood at the door. "I tried calling, but the lines are busy and I didn't have a cell number."

"No problem." Finn walked over. "Come on in."

"I'm ready to get started." He shoved his hands in his pocket. His eyes shifted around the department.

"Yeah. Great." Finn's voice rose. He pulled his keys out of his pocket and took his house key off the ring. "Here's the key. Help yourself."

"Great," Riley said. "Have a good day."

"Do you think you should've just given him a key?" I asked Finn when he stood up.

"Why not? Ben trusts him. He looks like he does a good job and I just want to get it done." Curiously he looked at me. "You're the first person to tell a stranger how safe it is around Cottonwood and no one ever locks their doors."

"True." I shook my head and rolled my eyes. "You do listen to me."

"Mmmhhmmm." He hummed and bent down to kiss me.

"I'm going to follow him out." Finn gestured after Riley. "I thought I'd run and see Dr. Shively to get a formal statement because she called earlier saying she was booked with patients, but would squeeze me in for a few minutes. Now more than ever we need to get her statement."

"Sounds good." I forced a smile, though my mind was numb.

Chapter Twelve

Instead of driving down to Ben's, which was only a short couple of blocks north on Main Street, I decided to take Duke and walk. Walking in the fresh spring air might clear my head and help me start to think logically. Not only had I thought about taking evidence from Frank Von Lee's room where he was murdered, I'd also already convinced myself that Mama was a killer when I knew deep in my bones that she wasn't. She might talk a tough game, but Mama was no different than any other red-blooded woman.

She had feelings. She was just better at shrugging them off and not letting the entire town see.

Duke and I took our time enjoying the spring sunlight on our faces. Why was it that the sun made everything so much better and the warmth put a little giddy-up in my step?

"Kenni! Kenni!" Viola White stood in front of her shop, White's Jewelry, next to Polly Parker. They were trying to open the tripod chalkboard sign. Polly gave it a swift kick and it popped right open.

"Maybe walking wasn't such a good idea," I said to Duke.

Duke trotted on over to Polly and Viola, knowing a good scratch behind the ear was imminent.

"Oh, Kenni." The words were so sympathetic but pretty as they flowed out of Polly Parker's plumped-up lips. Not a normal look for her, but it reminded me of Mama's appearance as of late.

Polly was a petite blonde that worked at the jewelry store a few days a week. She was what I'd call a hillbilly with money. On her daddy's payroll and on the arm of Mayor Ryland—though he was my daddy's age and Polly was a few years younger than me. I had uncovered their affair, which was the hot gossip for a few weeks but had since died down. Now seeing them together was no big deal. I still didn't understand what she saw in him.

"I sure don't think your mama is a killer." Polly drew her left hand up to her chest. On it was the biggest diamond ring that I bet Viola White had ever carried in her shop. "When Chance told me about Frank Von Lee, I had to call all the girls and let them know that we need to rally for Viv."

All the girls? She meant the henny-hens that were my mama's friends and Polly's mama's friends. Apparently, since Polly was dating Mayor Ryland, she'd also taken on the role of pretend wife with his friends.

"Yes." Viola swung the hot pink feather boa around her neck. Duke jumped up and tried to catch the floating feathers that'd wiggled loose from her flinging. "There's no way your mama could hurt a flea. She talks a mean game and she can get stuff done, but murder? Never." She gasped, making her five-foot-four frame seem so much bigger.

A few strands of pearls were wrapped around her wrist and she had a pearl ring on every single finger, though different in sizes and shapes. She was a walking billboard for her shop.

She pushed up her wide-rimmed black glasses with her middle finger before she raked the edges of her short gray hair.

"Who said Mama was a killer?" I asked. If Mama heard the rumors already swirling around, she'd never come out of the house.

"When I found out it was Frank, I knew that your mama had the most to gain or lose from his review. I mean..." Polly's shoulders did a weird wave as she flung that blonde hair of hers behind them. "It doesn't take a cop to put two and two together. If he liked her pot pie, she was going to be famous. If he didn't, she couldn't possibly ever cook again. Not to mention that last night at the end of the Shabby Trends show, I heard through the grapevine that Vivian was seen at the Tattered Cover looking awfully upset." Polly raised a brow. "Suspicious behavior if you ask me."

"Mmhmm." Viola's head nodded up and down. "Plus that." She pointed to the Cottonwood Chronicle box that was chained to the carriage light lamppost in front of her shop.

There were two photos of Mama on the front page. On one side was her coming out of the barbeque shack in Clay's Ferry, and on the other a close-up of Mama with her big shiner around her eye. I ran over and tried to jerk the newspaper container open, but I had to put in two quarters.

"I need fifty cents." I patted around my pockets. Edna Easterly sure did work fast in releasing this paper.

"Hold on." Viola White rushed into the shop.

I bent down to get a look.

"Edna." Disgust came out of my lips. "I can't believe her."

Viola ran over with the two quarters. I took them and pushed them through the slot. The clanking sound of the second quarter let me know I could open the spring door.

I pulled a copy of the paper out and stared at it. Mama wouldn't have let Edna take a photo of her with a black eye.

"How else did she get the black eye?" I swear there was a bit of sarcasm in Polly's voice. "I mean, really?"

"Really, Polly, my mama is not even on my radar." I curled the paper up and stuck it under my arm. "Come on, Duke!" I yelled out of frustration.

When I didn't hear the pitter-patter of his toenails on the concrete sidewalk, I turned around. Polly and Viola had their heads stuck together and were flapping their lips. They stopped when they saw me looking. Both of them shot their hands in the air and gave me the finger wave.

"Duke!" I screamed at my dog when he took off into a full sprint and made it to Ben's before I did. I opened the door of the diner and the bell dinged.

"Wow." My mouth dropped. It appeared as if there was a line for a table. "Business seems to have picked up," I said when I walked up to Ben, who was standing behind the counter.

Through the window I could see Jolee cooking.

"Business has been great. After the news of Frank's death, everyone has wanted to come here and ask questions about it. I only tell them what I know." He swiped the clean rag across the counter and stuffed some singles from a tip in his apron pocket.

"Ben Harrison. You of all people." This was nuts. "You know Mama and she's no killer."

"All I know are the facts." He turned around and threw the rag in the sink behind him before he grabbed a couple paper placemats and napkin-wrapped utensils. "What I know is that Frank Von Lee is dead and your mama was seen leaving the hotel upset. Then this morning she's front and center on the paper with a black eye. It all adds up. Plus I heard about the little fiasco from Clay's Ferry." He threw his hands up in the air. "Yesterday afternoon someone came in and was talking about it."

The kitchen door swung open and Riley Titan walked through.

"Oh. Sorry." He put his hands in the air with a surprised look on his face. "I didn't mean to interrupt. I just need my ladder. I was on my way over to Finn's and realized I left it here."

He looked around. Ben pointed back to the kitchen.

"I found it out here in the corner and had to move it out of the way this morning. I stuck it in the corner of the kitchen,"

Ben told him.

"Thanks, man." Riley offered a smile and disappeared back through the door. After I heard the back door to the diner shut, I walked over to Ben.

"Seriously, of all my friends," my head tilted to the side and I stared at him, "you're the one who I can't believe is acting this way. And there's no one who said Mama killed someone."

"It doesn't matter. You know gossip around Cottonwood. If they just think that something bad went on around here, they will come for the gossip." He gestured to the full diner. "I need the money."

"Can we talk somewhere a little more private?" I asked when I noticed there wasn't a single spot in the diner without a warm body in it.

"Sure. We can go in my office." He held up a finger for me to hold on and walked over to talk to a couple of the kids on his staff. They made eye contact with me and nodded.

I followed Ben into his office and shut the door behind him. "Shoot."

"What was said in the meeting yesterday when Frank Von Lee came in?" I asked.

"I greeted him. Like a good gentleman, I introduced Viv and then myself. Both she and I told him how happy we were to hear he was coming and you know," he shrugged, "we took turns kissing his you-know-what."

"How did he react?" I asked.

"He said it was his job and he loved to discover small-town recipes that bring light to the south. Some kind of light," Ben muttered. "Who knew that the expiration of his light would bring in this much publicity?" he asked with a chipper voice.

"Back to the questions." I found it odd that he was so upbeat.

I hated to play hardball, but this was my job and Mama's

life was on the line. I couldn't be in denial any longer thinking that I'd made all this up in my head. She definitely was the only suspect and the evidence was just mounting up against her. I'd never had such a clear-cut case. It was almost a little too clear-cut.

"Did he tell you his plans for the evening or what the plan was for today?" I asked.

Out of the corner of my eye, a shadow whisked across the office. My head jerked up and there was Poppa. He was milling around in the office. If he was looking around back there for clues, it saved me time.

"I'm going to look around in the kitchen," Poppa said and ghosted away.

"He said that he'd had a long day of traveling since he only traveled by train and that he wanted to just relax and read." Ben sucked in a deep breath and released it. "I mentioned that Nanette had a great supper, but if he was hungry, he could call over and get something for takeout. He never called."

"Did he eat anything while he was here?" I asked. "Was there anyone else besides Jolee cooking?"

"I offered him a couple of homemade cookies I'd made earlier in the day, but he passed. Jolee is the only one that's been in the kitchen since I fired Chef Mundy. Plus, I'd closed the diner after he left to prepare for today." He shook his head. "Really, I don't think your mama is capable of this, but it's awfully coincidental."

"Do me a favor. Don't give into gossip. Let me see what I can figure out. Let me do my job." I stood up. "I'll get back with you."

We headed out into the kitchen. Jolee pointed to the coffee maker. The steam rolled off of the freshly brewed coffee and the smell made my taste buds water.

"Do you mind if I take a look around?" I asked.

"The place is all yours." Ben poured himself a cup of coffee and one for me as well.

"Thanks," I said and offered a smile.

"I didn't find any sodium fluoroacetate." Poppa stood in the middle of the pristine kitchen. He was as baffled as I was. "If your mama had made a pot pie, then why is that in the trash? She'd never use a frozen dinner."

I looked into the bin. Before I reached in, I took a pair of gloves out of my bag and put them on. I pulled out a cardboard zip tab that you'd find on a premade frozen box. I dug a little deeper in the trash but didn't see a box to go with it.

"Ben?" I called. "Do you use any sort of frozen dinners here?"

"No," Ben said, offended. "Why on earth would you think that?"

"Jolee?" I asked.

"You know better than to ask me something that insulting." She smirked.

"I found this in the trash." I held the long thin piece of cardboard up in the air. I noticed half of a yellow price tag on it that I recognized from Dixon's.

"I have no idea where that came from." Ben turned to head back into the diner, seemingly unaffected by my find.

"How often do you take your trash out?" I asked, pointing to the trash can Poppa found the piece in.

"The ones by the counter are emptied a few times a day." He looked at the one by the pantry. "That one is rarely used because we don't prepare food there. So it might be once a week."

"Once a week." My mind rolled back to the people who'd had access to the kitchen. "Besides you and Jolee, who has been in here?"

"Your mama, me, Chef Mundy..." He stopped when I put

my hand up.

"Chef Mundy?" I asked, remembering that the last time I'd seen him, he was wielding a knife at Ben. "Where's he staying?"

"He has a place up in Lexington, but I was paying for him to stay next door." Ben's jaw dropped. "Oh, you don't think?" Ben's brows furrowed.

"I don't discount anyone or any motive." I took another look around until I was satisfied there wasn't anything else to see. "But he was staying at The Tattered Cover Books and Inn?"

"Do you think Mundy poisoned Frank to get back at me?" he asked and looked off into the distance. "I mean, he was right here."

"He was wielding a knife at you," I reminded him. "It's not like that's something you do to someone you care about."

"That's disturbing." Ben leaned back on the counter and crossed his arms. There was a concerned look on his face. "Crap." Ben dragged his hat off of his head and racked his hands through his hair. "I forgot to get his key. I gave him a key to the diner."

"Very disturbing." I patted my leg. "Come on, Duke. Bye, Ben," I said and walked out the back door.

The lid to the dumpster was propped up a little from all the collected trash from the businesses along this particular alley.

"You aren't." Poppa's nose curled.

"I am." I surveyed the dumpster, wondering how I was going to get up in it. I found a sturdy crate and dragged it over to the dumpster.

"This is why you have a deputy," Poppa reminded me as I started to climb in.

"Well, my suspect isn't my deputy's mother. She's mine." I put on another pair of gloves. Duke was busy smelling all the unique smells associated with a dumpster while I took my first step inside.

My feet sank into the bags and the odor was unforgivable. I gulped back a gag and started to sort through the bags. Ben's bags were black, so I grabbed all the black bags I found and threw them out of the dumpster. There were at least eight of them. I put them in a pile and headed on back to the office to get the Jeep to collect them.

The back streets took a little longer than just going down Main Street, but I was in no mood to answer questions swirling around the gossip mill about Mama. Though I did want to know how Edna got that photo.

There was no better time to ask her than on my walk. I dialed her number.

"Hi, Edna." I used my sweet Kenni Lowry voice. "It's Sheriff Lowry."

"Hi there." Her voice wasn't as happy to hear from me as I thought it should be. "I guess you're calling 'bout the article."

"Not so much the article, but the photo and how you got it." It wasn't against the law to take pictures, but there was no way she'd get a good shot of Mama without Mama's permission, and I'd bet my life that she didn't have it.

"I was on a walk and was just snapping pictures of our beautiful city," she lied.

"You mean that you heard about Frank Von Lee and you knew I'd go see my mama. You followed me to my parents' house to get the shot because you knew mama would open the door for me." It all clicked. "Am I right?"

"There's no law against taking photos." She loved to use the law to get her out of sticky situations.

"We do have an unwritten moral law," I reminded her. "Stay away from my investigation."

"You mean to tell me that you are investigating your own mama, not Deputy Vincent?" She was a sneaky one.

"Goodbye, Edna." I clicked off the phone.

Chapter Thirteen

By the time I'd walked back to the office it was almost time for me to go meet Mama at the matinee.

"People are going crazy around here." Betty told me something I already knew. She'd been fielding calls all morning and avoiding answering any questions that could fuel the gossip more. "And the national news has gotten a hold of the murder too."

"What?" There was something that we didn't need. After all, we'd just gotten through a big scandal from the death of the only famous person from Cottonwood, author Beryle Stone.

"There were a couple of calls on the messaging machine from them celebrity television shows asking about Mr. Von Lee's death. Then a couple follow-up calls after they'd gotten wind that it was a murder." Her right brow cocked, the right corner of her lip following. She finished, "They said they'd be on their way today and wanted to know what time you were holding a press conference."

"Press conference?" I asked.

Press conference? I noodled on the thought and got an immediate stomachache. I ran my hand over my ponytail and knew that I was in no shape to be seen on TV. No doubt they'd tear me to shreds if they did find out that my mama was the reason he was here and that she was really my only suspect at the moment. Though I wasn't discounting Mundy.

"Yep." Betty tapped away on her computer. "That means

you better get on over to Tiny Tina's and get your hair done, because they are coming whether you want them to or not."

I looked at my watch. I was already going to be late to meet Mama at the matinee and I had to find out what she was going to tell me about Frank.

"There's no time." The idea of being on camera gnawed at my gut. "I've got to go check out a lead," I lied. I didn't want anyone to find out that I was meeting Mama secretly. "Duke, you stay here." I flipped him a treat and headed out the door.

With Duke left behind at the department, I got into the Jeep, where Poppa was waiting on me.

"Where have you been?" I asked.

"Like you and Finn, busy trying to solve a murder." Poppa was frustrated and I could see why. "And I'm still running off any would-be criminals."

"What?" I jerked and looked at him.

"You think that little snot-nosed brat kids don't try to steal candy at Dixon's or sneak into Luke Jones's to see a movie? You better think again," Poppa scoffed.

"Oh. I thought that you just poofed away and back when I needed you." This whole gig with Poppa was strange.

"I'll always be here when you need me, but Cottonwood still needs me too." Poppa took pride in his new gig and I loved it. "After our earlier conversation, I put some more thought into the situation. I thought I'd keep my ghost eyes and ears open. Found out that I can still scare off any other crimes so you can focus on getting your mama cleared."

"Poppa, the only way we've ever gotten crimes solved, now and before, has been together." I reminded him how we'd always gone back and forth with ideas on different scenarios on how and why a crime was committed.

"I'm just not sure I can hang around and see the evidence pile up on her. I think it's best I continue to keep the rest of the town safe while you focus on finding the real killer." He was dead set on his reasoning and there was no way I was going to change his mind.

This time I could see that the investigation was so close to us that Poppa's objectivity he'd always been proud of was skewed, along with mine.

"I understand that this doesn't look good." I turned the Jeep on and drove down the alley, stopping at the stop sign. "But we have to process all the evidence and prove that Mama didn't kill anyone. You've always told me that solving a crime is like a mystery novel. The clues are there. We just have to pay attention to them to help solve the crime."

He sucked in a deep breath through his nose and let out a long deep exhale out his mouth. I turned out of the alley and then left on Main Street. I had to get to the dumpster behind Ben's and grab those black garbage bags.

"That frozen dinner pull tab really is on my mind. I know that pot pie can be frozen and I wonder who made a frozen dinner at Ben's." I had to get Poppa thinking about the case. It was the only way to get Mama off the suspect list. "Just think about Chef Mundy."

"He had access to the kitchen. He was very vocal about the diner and the noise the construction workers were making. Then he and Ben got into that argument." Poppa was coming around to the sheriff he used to be, putting the what-if scenarios together that made us such a great team. "There was that little moment he had too."

"When?" I asked, pulling up to the edge of the dumpster where I'd thrown the bags out.

"When Frank Von Lee came to the diner to meet with Ben and Viv, no one was in the back of the kitchen. Ben said Mundy still had a key," Poppa said.

"But they would've smelled the pot pie baking." It wouldn't

have been possible for Mundy to bake the pot pie then. "Though…" I stopped to gather my thoughts. "Ben did shut down the diner for his and mama's private meeting with Frank so he could get prepared for the real tasting the next day. I'm sure he ran some errands and Mama was who knows where that afternoon, but we do know her whereabouts later that day. I'm going to ask her where she was between the time she left the initial meet and greet with Frank and showed up at Lulu's. Back to Chef Mundy." I put my mind back on him as a possible suspect. "So Mundy could've walked over to the diner, slipped in the back using his key, baked the pot pie, and put the poison in."

"Yeah, but did anyone at the Tattered Book see him?" he asked.

"I don't know yet." I put it on my mental list to check out. "One suspect at a time. Right now meeting Mama to find out her exact whereabouts the entire day is my focus." I smiled and turned the Wagoneer off. "Mama is very sneaky. If she was going to be doing something and not want to get caught, she'd have been a lot more discreet."

"You're right!" Poppa's excitement grew. "I know she didn't do this. We've got to figure out who wants everyone to believe she did."

"Mama is vocal and would be a very easy candidate as a suspect since Frank Von Lee's entire visit was centered around her and that pot pie." I got out of the Jeep and opened the back door.

There was no time to go through the trash since I had to meet Mama, so I threw all the bags into the back of the Jeep.

On the way over to Luke Jones's movie theater, I gave Finn a quick call. When he didn't answer, I left a message letting him know that I might've found some evidence and I'd be sorting it at home. Conveniently I left out the part that it was trash. Smelly trash. Plus I wanted to tell him that I'd found out that

Mundy had been staying at The Tattered Cover Books and Inn, which might've put him at the scene of the crime. I was never comfortable leaving messages so detailed on an answering machine, so I left the message very vague.

The smell of warm buttery popcorn floated around me as I got out of the Jeep in front of Luke's house. A much better smell than what was inside the Jeep. We didn't have a movie theater in Cottonwood and it took us about forty-five minutes to get to a larger town if we did want to see a movie, so Luke and Vita Jones turned their basement into a makeshift theater. Granted, the movies were older (practically centuries), but the movie popcorn and candy made up for that.

"Afternoon, Sheriff." Vita Jones greeted me at the door with a big bag of fresh popcorn and a can of Diet Coke. "I figured I'd have it all ready for you when you got here. Your mama is up there sitting on the front couch."

"Thank you, Vita." I looked in the bag.

"Don't worry. I sprinkled some extra M&M's in there." She winked. "Besides, it sounds like you need that extra sugar with a murderer on the loose."

"We're working really hard on bringing some justice for Mr. Von Lee." I offered her a reassuring smile. "Thank you for the extra candy."

"I think your mama just got back from the eye doctor." Vita's brow rose. "She's got on a big pair of dark sunglasses."

"You know Mama," I said. "She's particular about getting wrinkles. Maybe the new spring sunshine is making her squint a little more today."

"That sunshine is welcome from me after the long dark winter we've had." Vita sucked in a deep breath and glanced over my shoulder out the window in the door behind me.

"I agree. Any sunshine is good for me," I agreed. "I'll see you after the movie."

"Groundhog Day. A favorite around here this time of the year." She handed a bag of popcorn to another movie-goer. "We're playing it a little longer this year since the groundhog predicted an early spring."

"I'm glad he did." I headed to the front of the theater.

Luke and Vita had gotten hand-me-down mismatched couches from various citizens of Cottonwood and placed them around the basement for movie-goers. There were different movie posters around the room. Today was a good day for a movie. The screen was pulled down at the front of the room, which was what made it a good day. Sometimes it was finicky and wouldn't cooperate when Luke tried to pull it down. On those days, Luke pinned up a king-sized sheet and played the movie.

Mama was curled in the corner of the couch, butted up to the arm. Her dark glasses still covered her eyes.

"Mama." I held the bag of popcorn out for her to grab a handful.

She waved her hand in the air, a hanky in her grip, declining the tasty treat. She used the corner of it to dab the edge of each eye. I wasn't going to fall for it. She wasn't crying. Mama had pulled the wool over my eyes one too many times.

"Did you see that gawd-awful newspaper?" She sniffed. "I'm going to call Wally Lamb and see what law Edna Easterly has broken because I know you'll tell me to let it go like you always do." She tried her best to mock me with her best follow-up sniff.

I eased down next to her and whispered, because I was well aware of the rubber-necking of the people around us who were trying to get a hint of our conversation. "You should let it go and let me do my job."

"Your job?" Mama squeaked. "You'll have me down there in that jail. In no time my hair will smell like that old fried catfish that Bartley Fry is so proud of."

"If you are guilty of something, then you need to tell me," I encouraged her. "I'm here because you said you had something to tell me."

The lights dimmed and the beginning of Groundhog Day started, and so had the sound of fresh popping popcorn, which let Mama and I talk a little louder than a hushed whisper.

"Go on." Mama threw her arms in front of her with her wrists up. "Cuff me. Arrest your poor ol' mama if you think I killed Frank Von Lee." She jutted them toward me a couple of times with her eyes squeezed shut.

"Mama," I whispered.

Her chin flew in the air; one eye squinted a little behind her sunglasses.

"I see you looking at me. Open your eyes and stop pouting." This was a position I never thought I'd be in.

"Pouting? You've accused me of killing a man. Your mama." She jabbed her chest with her finger. "Ouch." She quickly tried to rub out the hurt she'd caused herself. "I'm your mama. I brought you into this world. I gave you your name. I gave you everything you ever wanted. I paid for your college and now you are using that against me."

"What?" I jerked back.

"You are using the money I spent on your education against me by calling me a killer." She sobbed and threw her nose down into the hanky. "This was your grandfather's hanky."

Our louder-than-whispering conversation had spurred a few shushes from the crowd.

I grabbed Mama by her wrist and dragged her up and out of the basement.

"You mean Poppa?" I asked, dropping her wrist once we'd made it outside.

I'd never heard her call him my "grandfather."

"You know what I mean." She sniffed.

"Mama." I put my arm around her. "Give me something to go against all this evidence mounting up against you." The lines on my forehead wrinkled. I swallowed. Hard. "You went a little nuts in Clay's Ferry. You were seen at the hotel where Frank was staying right before Frank's time of death. Mind you, you were upset. You have a black eye, which makes me wonder whose fist you ran into. You're not your usual self. Give me something. Anything," I begged.

"Fine." All of a sudden the rush of tears dried. She pushed back her hair and jerked her shoulders back. She stood ram-rod straight.

"I wanted to look good. I'm not going to lie. I'd heard about someone doing those Botox parties at the condo complex on the river." I wasn't sure, but I think Mama tried to wiggle her eyes. Her forehead and brows were frozen. "I knew I was going to be doing newspaper interviews, radio interviews, and television interviews after Frank tasted my pot pie."

"Botox party?" I groaned, knowing this was probably something illegal and I'd have to add it to my list of things to look into.

"Yes. You go and pay your twenty-five dollars." She stopped when I put my hand in the air.

"Twenty-five dollars?" She and I both knew that was a red flag.

"Are you going to let me talk or keep interrupting me?" She crossed her arms, her face stern. She continued when I didn't answer. "I went a couple of days ago. I sat in a kitchen chair and they stuck me with needles and put this stuff in my face. I have to say that I was pleased at first. You know that phone call I made after we left Clay's Ferry?" she asked.

I nodded.

"I made an appointment to have more Botox injected. Late yesterday afternoon, I went back to get my eyes done again. The woman said she could make me look better and not blotchy. I was getting Botox around the timeframe you said Frank had passed. Then this showed up." She pointed to her eye. "I got on the internet and Googled. I think I got a bad batch of Botox or got something else."

"Mama, you had the Botox done around six?" This was good, but not perfect. I needed to know if she had given him a pot pie or not.

"That was the second time." She drew in a deep breath through her nose. "I went right after I met Frank because I just wanted to make sure I looked good on the television."

"That explains the eye. What about the food?"

"I have no idea how the food got there. I confess that I had an idea to make ribs like the place we went to eat in Clay's Ferry. I'd even gone as far as to go to Danny Shane's Dairy Barn to get some creamer to make the barbeque sauce thicker and spicier."

"Yes, they did have good ribs." I nodded.

"I didn't give Frank anything. I am guilty of going to the hotel. Nanette gave me his room number. When I went up there, I had planned on asking him if he'd rather have barbeque or the pot pie. He told me that he'd gotten the pot pie I'd sent over and was doing his review and I wasn't going to be happy." She pulled her lips tight. "I didn't take him a pot pie. I told him that I didn't even make the pot pie yet, but he grinned and told me that's what they all say once they get a bad review. I broke into tears and ran off. That's when I rushed back to the Botox party."

"Katy Lee saw you so upset after you'd run out of the stairwell." I made a note to ask Nanette if someone had dropped off a pot pie at the hotel and what the time was to see if it went with the timeline Finn and I had put together.

"Yes. I couldn't tell her that Frank told me he was going to write a bad review. So I did the best I could to keep it together. After I went to get my second injection, I went straight to the cooking class at Lulu's Boutique. In fact, I had a plan to take Frank that pot pie I was going to make in class after we were finished so he could see the first one wasn't mine. I swear." She put her hand up like Scout's honor. "Someone wanted him dead and they blamed it on me. Poor little ol' me." Mama sobbed into the hanky.

"I believe you." I put my hand on her knee.

"You do?" she asked. She looked up at me, her eyes dry as a bone.

Chapter Fourteen

I strongly suggested that Mama keep a low profile until I got the evidence processed and saw if any more leads came up. Time was not on my side, and I could feel it nipping at my heels like an angry dog. Poppa had disappeared, proving to be no help, angry that the evidence pointed straight at Mama with very little wiggle room.

I found Nanette in her office at The Tattered Cover Books and Inn, sitting behind the computer looking at all the news that'd found its way on the internet about Frank's murder.

"It's everywhere." Nanette's eyes grazed the top of her computer. Her reading glasses sat on the edge of her nose.

Purdy, The Tattered Cover's cat mascot, jumped up on the bookshelf behind Nanette and curled up on a pillow.

"May I?" I picked up one of the cat treats that was sitting on Nanette's desk.

"Sure." Nanette didn't even look up at me. She continued to tap on her computer.

"Here you go, Purdy." I put the treat next to her paw and ran my hand down her fur. She purred and took the treat.

She was a good cat. Nanette had a big sign posted and she told all the guests before they made a reservation that she had a cat. If they were allergic, they shouldn't stay, because Purdy had free reign of the place.

"Kenni, this has to be solved or no one will ever come back to Cottonwood." Nanette got my attention. "The food you found in his room was not from here. He didn't ask for food."

"Exactly how did you know about the food?" I asked since I knew I'd not disclosed any information to the public.

"Well...um...you know. Small town." She meant gossip and someone had let the cat out of the bag. That someone had to be Betty Murphy.

I turned around and looked over her shoulder. She scrolled down a Google page and from the looks of the links the media had published their online news a couple of hours ago.

"Betty," I said into the walkie-talkie and walked around the desk. "Can you please call the Reserve and let them know about Frank Von Lee's murder? Tell them to send some officers down here in case more of the media outlets try to get a scoop on the story. And please stop gossiping about it."

"Now Kenni, when people ask me things, I can't lie. It's not my nature." Betty made an excuse.

"Betty." I paused to make more of a point. "This is a murder investigation. We don't tell anyone anything until we have all the facts and killer in custody." I sucked in a deep breath. "Please make that call."

"Will do, Sheriff." Betty clicked back. "Also, Frank's agent and the Culinary Channel people called to say they were coming. Mayor Ryland has called an emergency council meeting for tonight at seven p.m."

"Thanks, Betty. I probably won't be back at the office this afternoon." I checked the time. It was almost three o'clock now and Mayor Ryland would want some sort of confirmation that our small town was safe and ease the citizens' fears.

"I'll let you know if I hear anything else," Betty said.

I clicked off and scrolled the volume down so I could talk to Nanette.

"This is going to explode all over the media. I mean," fear set on Nanette's face, "this is a big deal when someone famous dies. Remember the media circus from Beryle Stone? No one is ever going to want to stay here again. I'm going to be run out of business." She looked over my shoulder and out into the lobby, where a couple of guests were hanging out. "At least no one's cancelled their room today. We're full, and I feel like I'm going to need the money if we do have a backlash."

"This is why I'm here," I said to Nanette as I sat down in the chair in front of her desk.

It was the perfect opportunity to dig my heels in and ask her questions during her vulnerable state. I dug down in my bag to get my tape recorder and remembered I'd left it at the office, so I grabbed my paper and pen.

"I'm sure you hear that I've got a few leads. I'm asking everyone who was there at the time and wanted to know what you remember. And if you remember seeing mama here around that time."

"I don't recall. I guess I was getting supper ready for the guests." She busied herself with shuffling some papers.

"It's okay. I know that you talked to Mama. I also know that Mama asked you for Frank's room number." I held my pen to the paper.

There was a silence. I waited.

"Nanette." I eased up on the edge of the chair and leaned my arms on her desk. "I know that you don't want to rat on her and that she's my mama, but that doesn't mean I don't want justice brought for Frank's murder. Don't get me wrong, I'm going to try to find out everything I can and hope it doesn't point to Mama, but I'm the sheriff and I have to put all bias aside." She looked at me. "This means that you can tell me everything."

She nodded and took a deep swallow.

"Can you tell me about Vivian Lowry," I decided to use Mama's name to make it seem more professional, "coming in here on the afternoon of Frank Von Lee's murder?"

She nodded again. I took my arms off the desk and sat back a little.

"I'd much rather tell Deputy Finn if you don't mind," Nanette said in a soft voice.

I offered a tucked-in lip smile. Who could blame her? I didn't think about how this was going to make other people feel.

"Kenni!" Poppa appeared at the door. "Come quick!"

"I'll have Finn come by." I stood up, grabbed my bag, and headed out the office door.

Poppa stood at the door. I hurried over and looked out, forcing my mouth to stay shut. There were too many people around for me to risk talking to him.

"Chef Mundy." Poppa nodded toward a small black car. "He was here. He was leaving with a suitcase."

I tried to get the license plate number of the car, but Danny Shane walked past the front door with a ladder in his hands and blocked my view.

Malina Woody was behind the inn's desk. She grew up in Cottonwood and was what you'd call an old maid at the ripe old age of thirty-three. Mama was worried sick I was going to be a Malina Woody. She was a reader. I remembered going to the library when I was younger and seeing her there with her nose stuck in a book. She still walked down the street with a book in her face.

"Malina, y'all having some work done?" Saying her name got her to look up.

"I think we had some gingerbread lattice coming off and a few other things. Mr. Shane's been here the past couple of days fixing it for Nanette," she replied, flipping a page of the book she was reading.

"Did you get your hair highlighted?" I asked, wanting to get a little friendlier.

"I did, and a cut." She smiled and twirled around. Her long stringy brown hair had been cut into an asymmetrical bob that was completely out of her norm. "Do you like?"

"I do like." I really did. Those fancy haircuts weren't for me, nor did it fit my style of just throwing my hair up in a ponytail. I envied how cute she looked. It was a wonder Finn had found me remotely attractive since I rarely fixed my hair or wore makeup.

"I got it done down at Tiny Tina's." She smiled. "The only bad thing about having this kind of cut is that I have to go back every four weeks to trim it up or it won't lay right. Between me and you, I'm going to ask Nanette for a raise."

"Maybe I can help you," I suggested, knowing I probably couldn't and that Nanette really didn't want me around here asking questions.

After all, who wants the sheriff's department in their place of business twenty-four seven? The quicker we get this solved, the quicker she can have the inn back with no interruptions.

"I need a little information, and if you help, I'll be sure to tell Nanette how valuable you really are, because I can tell that you are smart and very observant."

"I was about to go clean room four, so you can follow me up if you'd like." She perked up even more. "Does this have to do with that man who was killed in room three?"

"It sure does. I'd love to follow you up." I leaned back a smidge and looked into Nanette's office. Her head was glued to the computer monitor. The coast was clear.

I waited for Malina at the bottom of the steps and followed her to the second floor where the rooms were.

"Room four, hmm." I played nonchalant. "I thought the inn's rooms were full."

"They are. Well," she stopped at the top of the steps and looked at me, "they were until a couple of minutes ago. This is his room."

"His room?" I asked, probing for some answers.

"That chef that Ben fired was staying here in room four." She pulled a key out of the cleaning bin she'd carried up with her and opened the door. She flipped on the light. "He had an open reservation and had pre-paid for a couple of weeks. He threw his key on the desk and said 'I'm out.'"

"You didn't know he was leaving early?" I asked, following her into the room.

It was a disaster.

"No. He didn't even ask for a refund either." Her brow cocked. "And it looks like he was in a hurry too."

The room was destroyed. The bed sheets were tossed on the floor. The trash can was overflowing. Dirty wet towels were strewn from the bathroom into the suite. The desk had crumpled-up pieces of paper on the top and on the floor around it.

"Malina." I put my hand out when she reached down to get the comforter and the rest of the bed covers off the floor. "I'm going to have to ask you to leave everything here and not touch anything."

"Huh?" Her head jerked back.

"Think about it." I was about to plant a new suspect in her mind, knowing she'd head straight downstairs and gossip a little. The gossip would make its rounds, and by the time it circled Cottonwood, Mama's name would be old hat. "Chef Mundy had a chip on his shoulder from getting fired."

I set my police bag down on the only clear spot on the floor next to the desk.

"Are you saying that he could've killed that fancy food critic? Because he was so nice. I couldn't imagine him wanting to do anything like that. He flirted a little with me." She tilted her head like Duke did when I asked him if he wanted to go for a walk or wanted a treat.

I wanted to pat her on her head and say good girl, but I refrained.

"You are one smart cookie, Kenni-bug." Poppa rocked back on his heels.

"I'm not saying anything," I said to her, because I didn't want her to misquote me, but whatever it was she heard was perfect. "But you might be right. And I can't let any evidence be thrown out or cleaned."

"This is unbelievable." Her voice was hushed. "He didn't seem like a killer when we talked in the kitchen. I mean..." She hesitated before she looked at me with a thin grin. "What can I do to help?"

"Not a thing. You just give me the key and your phone number in case I need to get a statement about your interaction with him, and I'll be sure to tell Nanette," I answered.

I held my hand out. She dropped the key in it. I put it in my pocket and then took out my phone. She rattled off her number and I put it in my contacts before she rushed out of the room and down the hall.

I walked over to the door and peeked around the door jamb, watching Malina's back end disappear down the steps. I pulled my phone out of my pocket and quickly called Betty Murphy at the department.

"Betty, it's Kenni." She did some umm-hmms on the other end. "I need you to get ahold of the judge and get me a search warrant for the entire Tattered Cover Books and Inn. And pronto."

There was a limited amount of time before Nanette got word I was up here going through the room. It was more unflattering news for the inn that she'd not welcome. She would want some sort of documentation allowing me to be in this particular room.

I snapped on some gloves and picked up one of the

crumbled pieces of paper off the desk. I ran my hand over it to straighten it out and left it on the desk. I did the same thing to a couple more pieces and noticed the handwriting was the same. I'd have to get a handwriting analysis to see if it was Mundy's, though I suspected it was since all of them were the same writing.

"Chicken pot pie," I read off the top of one, and then the next, and then the next.

One after the other, the text heading read "chicken pot pie." He had been making a recipe and it looked as though each one had a different seasoning.

"He's trying to figure out what your mama puts in her pot pie." Poppa stood in the door of the bathroom. "He's got all sorts of ingredients in here. And there's blood."

"Blood?" I dropped the piece of paper in my hand.

Before I made it to the bathroom, Nanette pushed the door open.

"Kenni!" She stomped. "Do you have a warrant for this room? Because if you don't, I've got someone who needs to stay here."

"It's on the way. And with blood in the tub..." I stood at the bathroom door. There was a deep red blood smear along the bathtub edge. "I'm not moving an inch."

"Blood?" She gasped and drew her hand up to her chest.

"I'm going to need all the paperwork for Mr. Mundy," I informed her and clicked on the walkie-talkie. "Betty, I need you to call Finn and tell him that we have another suspect. Tell him to find out anything and everything he can about Chef Mundy from Ben's."

Nanette went back downstairs. I quickly gathered the papers with the recipes and put them in evidence bags. I swept the room, snapping a bunch of photos.

"You know," Poppa was still studying the blood, "I'm pretty

sure the blood on the knives is Mundy's, because that looks like chicken parts in the tub. He seemed to be cutting up the whole, fresh chicken in the tub and probably cut himself on his own knives. But where did he cook the recipes?" He asked a great question. "If he did cook pot pie, then he might've made the one for Frank."

I took the evidence markers and set them around the room while taking photos. I took some swabs of the blood for evidence along with all the ingredients. I went through the trash.

"There's not any sort of frozen dinners in here," I said.

"He's a chef. He wouldn't lower his standards to frozen dinners." Poppa's eyes darted around the room.

"Mundy would have reason to murder Frank," I said to Poppa.

"I was thinking the same thing." Poppa looked out the room door. Apparently, the coast was clear because he kept talking.

I walked over to the door and shut it so no one would think I was talking to myself.

"Jealousy is a very powerful motive." Poppa referred to the second biggest motive for murder.

"You know, he yelled at Ben at the diner the other day saying he couldn't work in such loud conditions, but he was making basic things like biscuits and gravy. He shouldn't have had such a hard time." I looked around the room to make sure I didn't miss anything and picked up the mattress, pillows, and towels. "He might've been working on a pot pie recipe then and Ben didn't know it. He could've tried to take away Mama's thunder and when Ben fired him, he killed Frank out of anger at Ben. Though it looked like Mama did it..."

Poppa smacked his hands together.

"As long as he brought down Ben and the diner, he didn't care who he ran over, including your mama." Poppa's eyes lowered. "He was making the pot pie over here and he served it to Frank."

"Yeah, but if that's the case…" I hated that I always played the devil's advocate to Poppa's ideas. "Why did he leave everything here without trying to clean it up?"

Poppa scratched his chin. "Maybe he saw you downstairs and thought you were there to close in on him."

Nanette came into the room with the paperwork on Mundy I needed.

I grabbed my phone and called Betty.

"Betty, I need you to plug Mundy Brell into the computer databases and see what you turn up."

Chapter Fifteen

"Where are you?" Finn asked after I'd gotten back in the car and answered his call.

"I'm at the hotel. Where are you?" I asked.

"Chasing dead-end leads on this handicap sticker case." He reminded me that I'd completely forgotten to tell him about Mama's and had even forgotten to ask her about it. "Did you find anything out? Betty called to tell me that I need to check into Mundy."

"Since you are at a dead end, why don't I swing by and get you and Duke. I need to head to the lab in Clay's Ferry." It would be good to have him ride along with me. Not only to tell him the latest news, but just to be with him since we'd not been able to spend any time alone the past couple of days. "I'll tell you everything on our way over there."

"Not the kind of time I really want to spend with you, but I'll take what I can get since I hear tonight we have a town council meeting to go to," he said.

"I'll see y'all in a minute." Literally in a minute, I'd pulled in the alley behind the department where Duke and Finn were waiting.

"Hi." Finn opened the back door of the Wagoneer and let Duke jump in before he got in the passenger seat.

"Hi." I smiled, greeted him back, and leaned over to kiss him. "Pft, pft." I spit when Duke beat Finn to my kiss and stuck his head between us, licking me right in the mouth. "Hi, buddy,"

I baby talked Duke and rubbed his head.

Finn gave up and leaned back in the seat, tugging his seatbelt on.

On the way to the lab, I told Finn about Nanette and how she only wanted to talk to him.

"Before I'd gone to see her, I went to see Ben." I held the wheel with one hand and pushed Duke back with the other. He finally sat in the backseat. "The diner is hopping. He's got so much business because people are nosy. Then I found a piece of cardboard in the trash."

"I think I found it." Poppa chirped from the back. My eyes drew up to the rearview mirror where I looked back at Poppa. He was sitting right next to Duke with his arm draped around him.

"Go on," Finn encouraged me when I hesitated.

"And I can't help but think it looks like it's off one of those frozen dinners. I got the idea that maybe Mundy, since he still has a key to Ben's, came to the diner and cooked a frozen pot pie, put the poison in it, and gave it to Frank or left it for Frank to let Frank think it was from Mama." It was a stretch, but something to consider. "Not to mention, Ben was paying for Mundy to stay at the hotel while Frank was in town so he could be right there for work."

"Why would Mundy want to kill Frank?" He asked a very good question.

"Tell him about the hotel room." Poppa bounced in the seat. "You can't forget Mundy could've killed Frank out of anger for Ben firing him and wanted to put Ben out of business."

"That's what we need to figure out. You don't know the half of it." We were losing daylight hours. The country road between Clay's Ferry and Cottonwood was winding and trees covered the road like a bridge, only letting the sun through every few feet. "Mundy's room was a bloody mess. He was in the hotel room making food and there were chicken parts all over the bathroom." I pointed to the back of the Wagoneer. "That's why I'm going to see Tom Geary at the lab. I have a bunch of evidence I want tested for sodium fluoroacetate. Grab my bag and get the camera out. You'll see all the photos I took."

"This is why Betty called me to check Mundy out." He was adding everything up in his head.

"Yep." I gripped the wheel and took a sharp right into the driveway of the brown brick building where the lab was located.

Tom Geary was just locking up when we got there.

"Look at that old geezer," Poppa joked and ghosted himself out of the Jeep. "If I was still alive, we'd be doing some good investigating together." Poppa talked to Tom like Tom could hear him.

"Sheriff, what are you doing here?" Tom asked.

"Hi, Tom. This is my deputy, Finn Vincent." The two men shook hands. "I wanted to drop off some items to be tested for sodium fluoroacetate." I stuck my key in the keyhole of the back door of the Wagoneer to pull out the evidence bags from Mundy's hotel room.

"It must be important if you're personally bringing them." He took the bags from me.

"Just like her Poppa." Poppa puffed his chest out.

"You're just like your Poppa." Tom looked at me.

"That's what I hear," I muttered, trying not to look at Poppa "Do you think you can make these a priority?"

"You know it." He looked between me and Finn. "Nice to meet you, Deputy."

"You too." Finn gave the man-nod back.

"I hope he gets those run fast." I put the car back in drive and kept one eye on the road and watched Tom go back into the lab with the other.

It was probably too much to hope for, but I really wished he was going back in there to start the tests, but I knew he had a life just like the rest of us.

"What in the world is that smell?" Finn rolled down his window. The odor from the trashbags in the confined car had finally seeped out and stunk up the car.

Duke stuck his head in from the back and put it out Finn's window.

"Oh!" I started to laugh. "I totally forgot. The frozen dinner I was talking about, well, I found that piece of cardboard in Ben's trash. He said that he takes the trash to the dumpster, so I took all the bags out of the dumpster and put them in the back of the Wagoneer."

"Kenni, you are something else." Finn leaned over and kissed me on the cheek. "Let me guess, we are going to go through them."

"You are so smart." I teased and headed the Jeep back down the winding road into Cottonwood.

"Not that I'm grasping for straws to figure out another suspect, but you have to think it's super weird that Mundy would have all the ingredients in his hotel room that just so happened to be for the recipe Mama was making for Frank." That was just too much of a coincidence to me.

"We need to find the connection," Finn said. "I'm sure like every other business, the chef industry is pretty small once you get into it."

"I think we need to put him on the suspect list too." I gripped the wheel.

I'd always trusted my gut, and it was telling me Mundy knew Frank. But how? It was definitely something I was going to look into, but I first wanted to get the trash out of my car.

"Now what?" Finn looked at the time on his phone. "We don't have a lot of time before the meeting."

"I'm going to take you back to the office to grab your car

and go home to go through this trash."

Going into a council meeting armed with as much information as I could was my best shot. And I was hoping that I'd find something going through the trash. It might've been a long shot, but it was worth the effort.

Finn pinched his nose and playfully waved his other hand in front of his face. "Pee-eww. I'll be over to help."

"Thank you." I probably didn't say it to him enough, but I did appreciate all the time and effort he'd put into the duties of the office. "You really are a great sidekick."

"Hey now." Poppa chirped from the back. "I think me and Duke are pretty good too."

My eyes looked into the rearview mirror. I smiled. Finn turned around in the seat and looked into the back of the Wagoneer. Duke was curled up on the backseat asleep.

"What on earth are you smiling at?" Finn asked and turned back around.

"Nothing." I sighed. Eventually I knew I was going to have to tell Finn my little secret about my ghost deputy. I just didn't know when.

Chapter Sixteen

"And you're going through the trash already?" Finn smiled and plucked the handle of the gate that lead into my backyard open. His perfect teeth glistened in the early evening sun. My heart tumbled inside. "I thought I'd give you a few minutes to get Duke fed and settled, but you just dove right on in."

"I don't let the grass grow under my feet." I held up a piece of half-eaten Derby pie. "Shame." I looked at the pie and frowned. "Someone wasted a great piece of pie."

Duke ran over to Finn with a ball in his mouth. They played a little tug of war until Duke finally let Finn win and dropped it.

"I went to see Nanette on my way over here." He chucked the ball into the far right corner of the yard. Duke took off in a dead sprint.

"Oh yeah?" I looked up at him with my hand dug deep into one of the bags.

"She said that she didn't feel comfortable giving you a statement because she really liked you and your family. She didn't want to be the cause of any bad feelings." He picked up the ball Duke brought back and dropped at his feet.

"I can understand that, but I took an oath to uphold my duties as sheriff no matter what the cost. Including Mama's freedom." As hard as it would be to lock Mama up in jail, a murderer had to be brought to justice. "I'm just looking at all the other possibilities when it comes to strange things like Mundy's hotel room." I did take my responsibilities as the sheriff very seriously and I held the office above my relationships. It was part of the job.

"She confirmed that Viv asked for Frank's room number and that the occupant in room six complained about noise." He took his phone out of his pocket and with the pad of his forefinger scrolled through.

"They did?" I looked up at him.

"Yeah. She took the complaint." He held the phone out. "Here's a photo of the complaint."

I took his phone and read through it.

"It says here that they were in the hallway and that they didn't see Mama go into Frank's room." That was good. "And that Mama kept yelling 'it's not my pot pie.' Which is what Mama told me."

"And the time was around five forty-five. Which tells me that Frank had eaten some of the pot pie because he was already in the middle of writing that review." Finn walked over and pointed to the photo. He smelled so good, which made it difficult to concentrate. "The hotel guest said they'd called down to the office to complain and that's when Malina told them to come down and make a formal statement. As they were going down to the office, they passed someone with a tray and a drink that looked like someone from room service."

"But Nanette doesn't do room service," I noted.

"Right. The person with the drink knocked on Frank's door. They said a couple of words to each other before Frank took the drink, but they couldn't hear what they were saying." Finn had stumbled upon some really good stuff. "This makes me wonder if the empty glass we found on the desk was how he was poisoned and not the pot pie."

"I need to check if those labs from the crime scene are back yet." I'd put the glass in an evidence bag. Actually, I'd bagged everything. "But according to Max, the sodium fluorcacetate was found in the food in Frank's stomach."

Both of us stood there. We really wanted to find a way to prove that Mama wasn't the main suspect.

"After I left the hotel on my way over here, I stopped by the office to see if any of the labs were back and they aren't." Finn's eyes narrowed.

"If we find that frozen dinner box the zipper came from, maybe we can pull prints. I'm looking for the box." My gag reflexes kicked in when I pulled out more half-eaten food. "Thank goodness I have a lot more gloves."

"You are insane." Finn laughed and took a seat next to me. He grabbed a couple of gloves and slipped them on.

"I guess our next step until the labs come in is to talk to Mundy?" Finn asked.

"Yes. First thing in the morning I'm going to look into his past a little deeper," I said.

"Why would Mundy want to kill Frank?" Finn asked.

"I don't know. Maybe their paths crossed. Maybe to hurt Ben's business. Who knows." My body tensed. "Did Frank give him a bad review?"

"That's it!" Poppa appeared in the back of the yard with one of Duke's balls near his feet. Duke was bouncing around, wanting Poppa to throw his ball.

I gulped and prayed Poppa wouldn't throw it. Duke already looked like he had a head worm or something, bouncing and barking at the air—at least from Finn's standpoint.

"You can check out all the reviews Frank did. Anyone could find out where Frank was and kill him. There was no forced entry into the inn's room. Whoever it was, he opened the door. They fed him. He had to trust them enough to eat their food," Poppa said. He kicked the ball with his toe just enough to make Duke lunge for it.

"Is Duke okay?" Finn asked. "He's acting so weird."

"He's fine. Just been cooped up all day." I glanced at Poppa with an uneasy glare. "Another thing. How well did Ben know Mundy? Did Mundy and Frank know each other? Frank did let the killer in. He ate the food. I don't eat anyone's food I don't trust."

"I don't eat anyone's food if I haven't seen their kitchen." He surprised me.

"Really?" My thoughts darted to my kitchen, which happened to be a mess right now. "Speaking of food, I thought that maybe you and I could grab a bite to eat after the meeting."

He grabbed another bag of trash and opened it.

"That was a mess." He set the first bag of trash aside.

"While we look through the trash, we can listen to the first time Camille was interviewed at the scene. Maybe she said something that would point to Mundy as the killer," I suggested, because sometimes we did miss key evidence the first time. I dragged off my gloves and took the tape recorder out of my bag.

I pushed the play button. Camille began to tell her story from the time she was summoned to the Tattered Book and Inn.

We listened to her describe what had happened. "That's when he stood up, grabbed his chest and fell to the ground." She huffed a few times. "I think I'm going to be sick."

"That's when she went to the bathroom and got sick," I told Finn. The recording should've stopped there and gone to his interview with her, but it didn't.

The sound of paper came through the recorder. Finn and I both stopped.

"What's that?" he asked.

"I have no idea. I thought I stopped recording after she went to the bathroom, because I think you came in after that." I stopped talking to him when I heard my voice.

"There is nothing here that says Mama did him in." My voice sounded very nervous. "I shouldn't've ignored her behavior like I did."

There was a long pause before my big mouth started yapping again.

"I can keep the review and shred it. I can flush the pot pie or throw it in my bag. No one will immediately know he was eating it. Though Max will find it in his belly. It'll buy us time to get her a lawyer. A real lawyer, not Wally Lamb."

Shock flew threw me, and with the dirty gloves on, I reached over to grab the tape recorder.

"What was that?" Finn stood up and took the recorder before I could get it.

"It's not what you think." I shook my head and pulled the gloves off my hands. "I was just out of my head. Thinking out loud."

My words sounded really bad. It was when I'd been talking to Poppa after Camille had run to the bathroom. It sounded like I was going to hide all of the evidence against Mama. Very illegal, especially for a sheriff. Something I could go to jail for a long time for.

"You were going to hide evidence?" The look on Finn's face told me that he was upset and in disbelief.

"No." I reached out and put my hand on his arm. He jerked away and stood up.

"It sure sounded like it to me." His lips were open. His chest heaved up and down.

"I thought about it." The words rushed out of my mouth as I defended myself. My integrity. "I didn't do it."

"Thinking about it is almost as bad as actually doing it." His words stung. "What happens next time you think about it and follow through?"

"Are you serious?" My brows crunched as I watched him shove his hands in his pockets, along with the tape recorder.

"I'm dead serious, Kenni. You're the sheriff in this town.

You are the accountable one. Maybe you shouldn't be on this case."

There was a look of distrust and disgust on his face I'd never seen.

"You can't see the facts clearly. That's all I'm saying. You've spent the better part of this investigation looking for ways to clear your mama, not trying to find the real killer." His words stung, but he was right. "I'm going to get ready for the meeting. I'll see you there."

He gave me a quick kiss on the top of my head before he left. I could tell he was shocked and upset that I would've even thought about withholding evidence.

"You're human. She's your mama," Poppa reminded me.

Chapter Seventeen

"Are you sore at me?" Poppa hung on to the handle grip on the roof of the Jeep as I took the corner of Main and Oak on my way to the council meeting.

Duke's head hung out the window. He gave a few low barks as we passed by people walking on the sidewalk who seemed to be taking advantage of the wonderful spring night.

"What on earth would give you that idea?" I asked Poppa with a sour tone.

"You are driving a little erratically and..."

I interrupted, "You know what? I'm mad at me. I'm mad at me because I know better than to talk to you outside of the confines of my...um...our house."

My nerves felt like a bundle of live wires. Finn thinking I'd withhold evidence really upset me.

"Finn thinks that my morals have been compromised because of the conversation I had with you. I'm mad at myself for letting my guard down." I looked over at Poppa. "At some point I've got to tell Finn that I can see you."

"I'm not so sure that'd be good," Poppa said. "Then he'd really think you couldn't do your job."

"I love that you and I continue to solve crimes, but I can't let Finn think I'd do something illegal," I said.

"You didn't do something illegal. A thought's not illegal, or we'd all be in jail for wishing someone dead," he joked. When I didn't laugh, he said, "You only thought about it. Though

Deputy Vincent seems to be taking the moral high ground, the law is based on evidence, not what he believes."

I parked the Jeep behind Jolee's food truck. Duke ran up to her side door and gave a loud bark to let her know he was there, and like every other time, she opened the door with a tasty treat in her hand for him.

"Hey there." She greeted me with a hot cup of coffee. "Things sure have taken a strange turn since I went to help Ben."

"What do you mean?" I took a sip, looking around to make sure no one was around.

"Business has been booming. I told him that I had to do my food truck tonight and left him swamped. He even hired two new bus boys. Can you believe it?" She smiled. "I got my old Ben back."

"That's great." I brought the hot coffee to my lips. It was a much-welcomed salve for my troubled soul.

Out of the corner of my eye, I saw Finn walking into the basement through the door located at the side of Luke's house.

"I have to head up to the mall tomorrow. Do you want to go?" Jolee asked.

"I can't. I've got to check out some leads," I said.

Mundy was on my mind. I needed to get his history and fast. I also hoped Tom Geary would get back to me with some preliminary results from the items from Chef Mundy's room at the inn. "I better get inside." I turned and headed toward the door.

The crowd outside of Luke Jones's house had made its way into the basement. Cottonwood didn't have a traditional town-council room to meet in. Though we had a small courthouse, it was only used for things like car titles and taxes. It just had a small courtroom that wouldn't hold all the citizens that came to the council meetings. Most of the council meetings were about upcoming events and the budgets. Mayor Ryland loved to talk, and people came because they wanted to hear any gossip going on around town.

"You don't want to go in there." Poppa ghosted next to me and Duke. "They're planning to pull you off the case."

"What?" I jerked around and looked at him. "How could Mayor Ryland do that without telling me?"

"Shhh." Poppa put his finger up to his lips. "You didn't call him back like you said you were going to," Poppa reminded me.

I glared at him, my eyes narrowed. It looks like I made my own bed and now it was time to lie in it, like the old saying went.

"There's not much you can do about it now. You've got to go in there and be smart. Remember not to let your mouth override your tail." He shook that finger at me. "It might not be a bad thing to get pulled."

He was right. I had to go in there levelheaded and listen. Not fly off the handle.

"How so?" I questioned him.

"You could do more snooping around and really dig deep without that uniform on." Poppa did teach me the trick that people talked more when I had on street clothes and not the official sheriff uniform.

The theater had been transformed from full of comfy couches to full of the rickety old fold-out chairs that formed rows facing the front of the room. The movie screen had been rolled up to the ceiling and replaced by a wooden podium where Mayor Ryland would preside over the meeting. Too bad the popcorn machine had been put away. I'd have gotten a bag and thrown pieces at the mayor as he tried to pull me off the case.

Mayor Ryland was bent over by the podium whispering into Finn's ear. His slicked-back salt-and-pepper hair was perfectly coiffed. His jaw tensed underneath his manscaped goatee as he spoke. His eyes swept up past the heads of the citizens sitting in the chairs and focused on me. His lips moved quickly before he stood up and tugged down the edges of his suit coat. Finn took a step back and turned his head, looking straight at me. Our eyes met. He mouthed "I'm sorry."

He closed his eyes and when he opened them, he focused on something else in the room. I sucked in a deep breath, pulled back my shoulders, and took the first step into the lion's den.

Too bad Duke had no idea he was trotting into enemy lines. He accepted every single head pat on our way up the middle aisle to find my seat right next to Finn.

"You aren't going to like what the mayor is going to propose." Finn had enough decency to think he was warning me.

"Finn." I gave one of my best southern grins. Poppa's head popped over Finn's shoulder. He had a big grin on his face too. "I'm not the new face around here. You are. I've seen what Chance does when things don't go his way. I've borne the brunt of his dislike for a few years now, so I'm sure he's going to suggest I be taken off the case."

"Because of your mama." Poppa nodded. He knew what they'd said from his ghostly eavesdropping.

"Because my mama is tied to the investigation," I repeated.

"And because you don't have the right mindset to remain unbiased," Poppa continued.

"Because he thinks I don't have the right mindset to remain unbiased." I kept my eyes on Finn and my peripheral vision on Poppa.

"He also thinks Finn needs to distance himself from you and Finn should run against you for sheriff in next year's election." Poppa's words stung me more than Finn thinking I'd done something to damage the badge I wore so proudly.

"Not to mention," my voice cracked, "he wants you to distance yourself from me personally so you can run against me in the election."

It was no secret that Mayor Ryland wasn't my number-one fan. But I couldn't please everyone.

"Kenni," Finn put his hand on my knee, "I'd never..."

"Order!" Mayor Ryland banged the gavel on the wood podium. "Good citizens of Cottonwood, it's time to bring things to order."

"Kenni," Finn whispered. "You know that'll never happen."

I offered a weak smile. Finn truly was amazing, and even though I was in a tight spot, I knew I was very lucky to have him on my side.

"We called this emergency meeting," Mayor Ryland spoke after the crowd hushed, "because it's come to my attention," he looked directly at Finn, "that Sheriff Lowry is in a very compromising position given the nature of the suspects in our latest murder."

The gasp of the citizens behind me broke the polite silence in the room, forcing Mayor Ryland to bang the gavel again.

Come to his attention? I wiggled my foot around as it dangled from my crossed legs. I tried to remind myself that it was a strange position to be in, but I knew I could keep the case from my personal life. Chance was probably right. The town wouldn't see it that way. It was going to be interesting to see how this all played out.

"I'm sorry, Sheriff." Chance offered an insincere apology. The smirk on his face was all too familiar to me. "We," he gestured to the council members sitting behind him that included Myrna Savage, Peter Parker, Ruby Smith, and Doolittle Bowman, "feel it's best that Deputy Vincent take the lead in the case since your number-one suspect is Vivian Lowry, the sheriff's mother."

"Well!" The scream from the back caused everyone to turn around. "Doesn't that just take the cake!"

Mama stood in the back with her big black shiner on

display for everyone to see.

"I didn't kill no one!" She stomped up to the center of the room. I swear I heard people shudder. I know I did. "If you think that, then you can cuff me right now."

She stopped in front of Finn and threw her wrists out in front of her like she'd done to me earlier in the day, almost in the exact same spot in fact. Finn looked between Mama and me.

"Order!" Mayor Ryland banged the gavel and pointed it at her. "You will take a seat before I have Deputy Vincent arrest you for being a public nuisance."

"Arrest me, you big oaf!" Mama had just called the mayor stupid. I braced myself.

"Don't you be calling my fiancé an oaf!" Polly Parker jumped up from the front row.

"Fiancé?" Myrna chimed in. "Did she say fiancé?" she leaned over and asked Doolittle.

Doolittle nodded.

"Err..." Polly's pale face reddened. "Um..." She took a couple of steps back to her seat. Mayor Ryland's chin hung to his chest. "Chance," Polly pleaded in her little girl voice. She didn't care what he thought, because she went right on. "Yes. Chance and I are going to be married." She beamed. Her big white horse teeth appeared as her open-wide grin spread across her face. Her hands were clasped behind her. Her body twisted right and left. "This is our official engagement announcement. Our wedding is going to be the biggest event Cottonwood has ever seen."

Polly looked around the room before she sat back down on the folding chair.

Mama looked at me and I rolled my eyes. It was just like a council meeting to turn to gossip. Edna Easterly pushed off the wall and started snapping photos of the mayor's face and of Polly, whose eyes were glaring at Chance as though they were having a telepathic conversation.

"People, my personal life is of no concern and has no bearing on what the council and I are trying to do tonight." He spoke with an even tone. "Polly Parker is going to be the next first lady of the town. She's right. We are going to have everyone at our wedding."

Polly was all giggles now. She sat up and held her hand in the air, showing off the big diamond I'd seen on her hand the other day. No doubt they'd gotten a discount from White's Jewelry since Polly worked part-time down there for Viola.

"Back to business." Chance tried to get the community to stop congratulating Polly.

I couldn't help but notice Pete Parker's—Polly's father and ex-best friend of the mayor—face. The more his jaw tensed, the redder his face got. It was just hearsay, but I'd heard over a hand of Euchre that after Pete found out about the mayor's and his daughter's secret love shack out in the woods, Pete and Chance had pretty much beat the poo out of each other. Chance had been Polly's godfather, and from what I'd heard, Pete told him that he wasn't no godfather, he was a sick old man that was making his daughter the laughingstock of the town. He'd even tried to get Polly to break it off, but she moved out and into the mayor's house. By the look on Pete's face and the lack of communication with Polly or Chance, I'd say the gossip was pretty close to being true. Unlike Mama killing someone.

"Can I have your attention?" I jumped to the stage and took the gavel from Chance. I gave it a quick couple of bangs. "You don't have to go back to your seats, but I do have something to say."

"You tell them, Kenni." Poppa was nose to nose with Mayor Ryland. "Don't you dare back down from your position while he waltzes in here to take over your office. I'm not so sure that wasn't his plan this whole time."

"There is more than one suspect in the case of Frank Von Lee. I do see how this looks like a conflict of interest for me." I cleared my throat. "I'm more than happy to let Deputy Finn Vincent take the lead on this case and use my expertise about our town and our citizens to help him. There are plenty of other cases I can be working on. Which brings me to a scam going around Cottonwood. There is someone distributing illegal handicap tags. If you or someone you know has a pink handicap tag, please call the sheriff's department. The only way to get a handicap tag is through the county clerk's office at the courthouse."

"Wait." Poppa ghosted over to me. I saw his eyes, large glittering ovals of repudiation. "You can't just lay down like that. You have to be on the case. You have to figure this out. You're the sheriff."

Before I could say anything else, Mayor Ryland jerked the gavel out of my hands and beat it on the podium, making my decision official.

"Kenni." Finn put his hand out to stop me when I stepped down and into the crowd.

"It's okay, Finn." I offered a smile. There was more behind the smile than he knew. Now I felt a little freedom to investigate as I pleased without being watched.

"Come on, Duke." I grabbed Mama by the elbow and dragged her down the aisle alongside me and Duke. She didn't need to be in here running her mouth and getting herself deeper in trouble. I didn't need to stay in there and listen any longer. I'd come to say my piece and now I had a job to do.

"Can you believe about the mayor and Polly getting married?" I shook my head and pulled Mama closer to me. I didn't want to talk about what I had planned to get her off the hook or the other case I was referring to.

"Did you see how she was dressed?" Mama seemed more

than happy to get the heat off of her. "I reckon he likes her dressing like a hooker."

I threw my head back and laughed.

"I love you, Mama." I tugged her even closer. "Let's go get a cup of coffee from Ben's."

Chapter Eighteen

The next morning I woke up in a foul mood. Not only had Finn tried to call several times, he'd even stopped by. Even though I told him it was okay, it really wasn't. I'd already had my ego bruised and needed to set that aside, but I needed a day to process it. He wasn't as familiar with Cottonwood and he wasn't in the gossip circle like I was, which was going to make it hard for him to get some little tidbits of information that I'd always found helped investigations.

Was he trying to get ahold of me so bad because he wanted to scold me for my words that were just words on the tape recorder? Or was he feeling bad that he'd taken the case right out of my hands and never once tried to protest it? If it was an emergency, dispatch would've called me, so I ignored him.

It wasn't until around three a.m. that I'd finally fallen asleep. Not a peaceful sleep. It was riddled with nightmares that included some weird things like being chased by a big diamond ring that lassoed itself around me. After the ring caught me, Finn was at the ready with a pair of handcuffs and hauled me down to the jail cell, which I had to share with Mama and her striped prison jumpsuit. I finally woke up after Frank Von Lee slid a plate of chicken pot pie between the bars of the jail. He was laughing the whole time, telling Mama and me that it was our turn to eat the poisoned food so we knew exactly how he felt.

That was enough to jar me awake. My phone next to the bed showed that I'd missed a phone call from Betty Murphy. She didn't leave a message. I pulled the covers off and slipped my feet into my slippers and grabbed my sweatshirt.

"Let's go potty," I called to Duke over my shoulder as I tugged my sweatshirt over my head.

On our way down the hall, I called Betty back, flipped on my coffee pot, and let Duke out into the backyard, but not before looking to see if Finn was back there.

"Kenni," Betty whispered in the phone. This wasn't like her.

"Are you at the office?" I asked, wondering why she was so quiet.

"Yes," she answered hesitantly.

"You can talk to me. I'm still the sheriff and will be coming into the office this morning." I took a mug out of the kitchen cabinet and waited for the coffee to brew. "I've got other cases to work."

"I wanted to let you know that I put those seed packets in the planter on your porch where you asked me to put them," she said.

"Are you feeling all right?" I asked her.

"Yes. Finer than frog's hair. Now, go get those seeds and start to water them so they can grow. You have limited time with this one," she said.

"Betty, are you talking in code?" I asked.

"Yep. That's the planter." She could've just said that in the first place. "A little fair warning. The press and media are camped out in the alley in front of the department."

"I'll deal with it when I come in." I groaned, knowing I was going to have to get all gussied up to have my picture taken and be interviewed by the media. "Can you please call Finn and let him know that he needs to be there to answer questions since he's in charge of the case?"

"Sure thing, Kenni." Betty clicked off.

I walked to the front of the house and opened the front

door. There was a planter on the small concrete slab full of a dead fern that I'd planted last summer and didn't bother taking out for the winter. It didn't go unnoticed by Mama. Every time she came over, she liked to remind me that there was a dead fern on my front porch.

When I opened the door, there was a corner of paper sticking out from underneath the planter. I looked both ways down Free Row to see if anyone was out before I picked it up, because you never knew who was watching these days and apparently whatever Betty had stuck under the planter was private or secret.

I tipped the planter up on its edge and pulled the folded paper out. When I got back in the kitchen, I put the paper on the table and let Duke in. I poured myself a cup of coffee and sat down, dragging my legs up underneath me.

I opened the paper and flattened it out in front of me. I sipped my coffee and read through all of Mundy's background check. He'd been kicked out of many restaurants. And there was a connection between him and Frank Von Lee. It just so happened that Mundy had been one of Frank's students in a New York culinary class. By the looks of the report, Frank had kicked Mundy out of the class. The last culinary school he'd attended was the one where Ben Harrison had graduated where they'd been classmates.

After Mundy had graduated, he went to work at Le Fork, a nationwide chain that held classes for the common folk like me. He'd worked there until a month ago.

"Where was he between four weeks and a week ago?" Poppa stood by the counter next to the coffee pot. He sniffed the steam. "I sure would love a cup."

"I'm going to have another." I stood up and refilled my cup. "So I guess you're not mad at me anymore."

"I was never mad at you." He looked out the window. "I just

don't understand why you gave up so easy."

On my way back to the table to finish reading the paperwork Betty had snuck over, I filled up Duke's bowl with food and grabbed my phone.

"I didn't give up. I'm using my brain." I scrolled through and hit the call button when I found Jolee's name. "I can still look into the murder. Only now all eyes won't be on me." I shrugged and put the phone up to my ear. "I don't have to make official reports unless I find something."

"Which we will." The color came back to Poppa's face. "You're still going to get your mama off the hook."

"Yep. Thanks to Betty." I eased back down into the chair, pulling my legs back up.

"I was going to call you this morning." Jolee answered the phone without saying hello.

"I beat you to the punch." I said. "I've got a quick television press conference this morning."

"Press conference?" She interrupted. "Ooh la la."

"Whatever. Anyways, I wanted to know if the offer still stands to go shopping."

"You mean to tell me that I can drag you forty-five minutes from here into Lexington, shop for a few hours, and then drive forty-five minutes back?" she asked with a hint of caution in her voice. "Because you want to get all dolled up for the TV?"

"No," I said flatly. "I want to go after the press conference."

"Fine. If I have to settle, then you have to buy a cute pair of shoes today," she said, driving a hard bargain.

"Are you serious?" I asked.

"Yes. I'm tired of you thinking that every outfit goes with cowboy boots." She laughed.

"They don't?" I asked, setting her off into a firestorm of how I needed to step up my fashion game. "I'll drive."

"What? You don't want to be seen in the food truck?" she

asked.

"I'm sure smelling like food isn't good for my fashion sense either." I took a drink of coffee. "Just joking. I don't mind driving, besides, I want to go to Le Fork."

"Oh, are you planning on cooking a romantic supper for a special someone?" she asked.

"No." I hadn't told Jolee about the latest setback in my relationship with Finn. I looked around for a quick kitchen tool I could purchase there. "I'm thinking about getting a French press."

I hoped my lie wasn't too far-fetched since she knew I loved coffee.

"I can show you the best ones," she squealed.

I probably should've realized anything with food would get her all worked up.

"I'll be over in an hour." I hung up.

"What's on your mind?" Poppa asked.

"It says here that Mundy taught classes there up until a month ago." I tapped the paper. "That's about the time Ben and Mama got word from the Culinary Channel that Frank Von Lee wanted to come try Mama's pot pie for the show. They didn't give Ben a specific date, but you know how fast news spreads."

"Mundy quit his job and came into town to work for Ben while Ben took care of the show gig." Poppa was right on track with what I was thinking.

"I was in the diner the other morning when Mundy was screaming about the construction work and how loud it was. Ben said to Mundy that Mundy jumped at the chance to work for Ben since they knew each other." My brows cocked. I took another sip.

"It would be easy to find out about or get Malina to talk about Frank's arrival. Mundy is smart, so he probably checked the only two places to stay in Cottonwood. Malina probably told him because he flirted with her."

"It doesn't seem like much flirting was needed to get information from her," Poppa said.

"And Mundy's room was right next to Frank's." It was the small details that helped solve a murder.

"Did Malina let Mundy cook in the inn's kitchen?" Poppa asked. "The pot pie that Frank was eating was in a dish, not a cardboard frozen-dinner container."

"So it's safe to say that the container thing is probably not related to the murder?" I stared at Poppa.

"I'd say we go on what we know and keep it in the back of our minds, but not focus so much on it." He slipped away.

It was so amazing how much I'd learned from Poppa when he was living and was still learning from him from the great beyond now.

Here was what I knew. Mama had the most to lose from a bad review, but the evidence pointing at her was just too obvious. Mundy, on the other hand, made himself obvious by fighting with Ben. Which I couldn't help but think was his plan all along so Ben would be out of the kitchen and Mundy would be able to replicate Mama's recipe, once again making Mama look like the killer.

Mundy had the greatest motive. Mama could get over the embarrassment of a bad review. After all, she was a southern woman. But Mundy was a scorned chef with a big ego that couldn't graduate from one of the biggest culinary schools in the United States. I had to believe that followed him to any reputable job at the fancy restaurants where he wanted to be the head chef.

Someone at Le Fork had to know where he was. He'd been employed there the longest. Surely he'd made some friends.

Chapter Nineteen

When Betty said that the media was camped out in the alley in front of the department, I didn't imagine truly camped out. But there were several white vans with television equipment on the top and some big satellites, their station's names printed on the side.

There were at least ten that lined from one end of the alley to the other end. On The Run, Jolee's food truck, was parked in my spot next to the dumpster in front of the department door. I pulled the Wagoneer up to the building and parked tight to Jolee's truck so not to block the alley in case there was an emergency.

"That's the sheriff," I overheard one of the reporters telling her videographer.

With a quick check of the lip gloss I'd put on before I left, I got out of the car.

"Look at you." Jolee grinned. "If only we had different shoes." She jerked a scowl when she noticed I'd put on my cowboy boots.

"At least this is a new shirt." I referred to the brown sheriff's uniform shirt and brown pants. "And the hair is down." I wiggled my brows. "I wasn't going to get caught looking like the last rose of summer."

When Betty had mentioned the media this morning, I had to take that extra time to actually put on makeup and fix my hair.

"Good morning," I greeted the crowd and everyone rushed over. "I'll be more than happy to take a few questions after I give a brief statement."

In the distance, there was a feather swaying in the air and rushing towards the department. It was attached to Edna Easterly's fedora. She scurried to the front of the media with her pen and pad in hand.

"As you know, we are investigating the homicide of Frank Von Lee. We are working on several leads and interviewing several suspects." "Several" was a bit of a stretch when we'd only interviewed Mama. Out of the corner of my eye, I saw Finn's Charger pull up. It was time to include him and the best way to ease into talking to him since our little spat. "I've handed the lead investigation over to Deputy Finn Vincent."

He walked up, not taking his eyes off me.

"Deputy Vincent will be more than happy to answer a few questions." I'd caught him off guard. I glanced over at Jolee and her eyes were big and round, darting between me and Finn.

His eyes softened when he stepped up next to me. He bent down and whispered into my ear, "I'd love to see you tonight."

"I'd love that too." My heart melted.

"Good," he whispered and straightened up. His eyes grazed over the media and he pointed to one of the reporters with her hand up in the air.

"This has really been a bad couple of years for Cottonwood." Her voice boomed above the crowd. "Do you think it's time for a change in the sheriff's department?"

"Change?" Finn asked. I fidgeted next to him.

"The community seems to be under a black cloud of crime. It's strange that crime was rare or actually practically nonexistent until the second year of Sheriff Lowry's term. Do you have anything to say to that?" she asked and held a small tape recorder up in the air.

"Actually, the couple of crimes you are referring to, as well as Mr. Von Lee's murder, are all isolated incidents. There is no crime spree or serial killer in Cottonwood. Cottonwood is safe. Safety is Sheriff Lowry's main concern," Finn stated flatly, not giving the reporter any more time. He pointed to Edna. "Edna."

"Is it true that Sheriff Lowry's mother, Vivian Lowry, is the only suspect in the murder of Mr. Frank Von Lee?" Her brows rose.

"This is an active investigation and right now everyone related to the reasons Mr. Von Lee is in Cottonwood is a suspect." He answered it with such an ease that I even believed him.

"Is the reason Sheriff Lowry is letting you take over the lead because her mother is the number-one suspect?" another reporter shouted from the back.

"There are only two people in our department, Sheriff Lowry and me. The sheriff needs to focus on the entire community, and while this is an isolated event, I'm going to handle it while she takes over all the other aspects of the job." He sure was good with words.

I touched him on the arm because there didn't seem to be any real questions about the case other than about me and my mama.

Finn stepped aside.

"I'd like to thank you for coming out, but we're going to have to ask you to clear the alley. It's not only illegal, but hazardous in case an emergency vehicle needs to drive down." I held my hands in the air. "We will put out a notice of when our next press conference will be. Thank you."

A few more questions were shouted out, but nothing that stopped us from going inside.

Betty's phone lines were lit up and blinking.

"It's going to be a long day of questions." Finn smiled

thinly.

"You're going to do just fine." I patted him on the back. "I'll make sure to have a few beers ready for you tonight."

"I'm glad you agreed to see me." His eyes were as sincere as his words. "I've missed seeing you."

"I've missed you too." It was like no one else was in the room, until Jolee interrupted.

"Okay, lovebirds, we've got to go. I've got to get her out of those shoes." She shoved between us.

"Huh?" Finn's brows furrowed.

"I told Jolee that I'd go shopping with her." I left it at that, not wanting to tell him or her my real reason for heading to Le Fork. Maybe I'd have some solid leads for him tonight when he came over.

Within five minutes, Jolee and I were in the Wagoneer and heading the forty-five minutes to Lexington.

"How's things going with you and Ben?" I asked, hoping that things had gotten better.

"He's still a little on edge, but he's letting me have control of the kitchen." She sounded much better than the last time we'd talked about it. "It's the strangest thing. Business has picked up since Frank's death."

"How well did Ben know Mundy?" I snooped.

"He said he didn't know much about him since they'd gone to school. He's just waiting for Mundy to come in and collect a paycheck for the few hours he was there because he said Mundy is hard up for cash." She stared out the window. "Enough about all that stuff. I've got my best friend back for a while."

She turned in her seat to face me.

"It looks like you and Finn are doing okay." I didn't have to look at her to know she was smiling big.

"He's a really good guy." A happy sigh escaped me. "But I'm missing doing my job."

"Nothing a little shopping won't help." She snickered.

It was so nice to spend some time out of the office and have girl time with Jolee. With a little gossip and a lot of laughter, we parked in the mall parking lot in no time. Jolee didn't waste any time we had. She was out of the car and into a boutique before I could get my seatbelt off.

"Isn't this great?" Jolee held a short-sleeved lace shirt up to her chin. "I think this would look great with a pair of jeans or pants. It'd even go with those cowboy boots."

I stared out the window of the shop, across the parking lot and at the Le Fork store.

"Kenni?" Jolee called my name. "Yoo-hoo, Kenni."

"Yes." I flipped around and smiled.

"Did you hear me?" she asked. Her blonde hair was actually fixed today. Normally she had to pull it back or she wore it in a cascading ponytail down her back, or in two with one down each shoulder. She crunched her nose. Her freckles came together, giving her an instant tan. "So?" She held up a top in front of me.

"Yes. It looks good on you." My mind was wondering how I could leave Jolee here and get over to Le Fork to snoop around.

"Not me. You." She shoved the hanger at me. "You didn't really want to come shopping, did you?"

"Of course I did." I held the shirt up to me. "Looks good?"

"Yes." Her voice was flat.

"I'll take it." I held it out to the sales lady.

"You're about as much fun as my mom," Jolee said.

I sat down on the sofa in the fancy boutique. "This just isn't me." I looked around the pink-and-cream-striped wallpapered shop. The chandeliers even had light pink bulbs with tassels dangling from the center of each one. The lighting made every piece of clothing and color look good on anyone. There were high-back chairs and long fabric ottomans positioned around the shop just in case someone was so exhausted walking around looking at the expensive clothes they had to sit and rest

"I like it. I just don't have anywhere to wear that." I pointed to the sales lady who'd walked away with the top.

"Finn." Her brows rose.

"That's not so good." It was time to let her in on what was going on if I was going to get over to Le Fork.

She hesitated. She blinked in bafflement and sat down next to me.

"What on earth happened? What did you do?" she asked, sure that it was my fault.

"Why would you assume that it's me?" I asked.

"Because that man adores you. When he comes to get a coffee or food, he always talks about you." She stared at me. "So what happened?"

"Mama happened." My voice was flat and followed up by a big long sigh. Just as if mama knew I was talking about her, she texted me. I held the phone in the air. "Mama. She must be feeling guilty because she's insisting I come for supper tonight. She's making my favorite."

I tucked my phone back in my pocket.

"At least she's trying." She looked off as though she were remembering something. "I thought she loved him."

"She did, until he got me kicked off her case." I put both of my hands on my knees and stood up. "Let's walk."

She nodded.

"Can you just hold those for a few?" Jolee asked the sales lady before she followed me out of the shop.

The morning had already turned into the afternoon. The outdoor mall was packed. It was one of those places where all the entrances to the stores were accessible from the outside. The parking lot was in the middle. There were little cafés and coffeehouses along with a few restaurants located around the mall.

"Don't these people work?" I had to turn to the side as we started to walk down the sidewalk in order to not get knocked down by a group of laughing women.

"You are so grumpy today." Jolee knew me better than probably anyone. "Spill it."

I pointed to the coffeehouse.

"Yeah, I could use a cup." She shoved past me and went inside.

The coffee smelled fresh and hopefully it would help clear the cobwebs on my feelings about Finn. I felt like my emotions were hindering me from working the case, even though I was off of it.

We ordered a couple of cups and took a seat against the wall at a table for two.

"Can you believe Ben's?" Jolee looked to be making small talk until we got comfortable to discuss why I'd brought her in here.

"The pick-up in business?" I asked.

"You know he was afraid business was going to die, but it's just the opposite." She laughed. "No joke. The news of the famous Frank Von Lee's death has made Ben's famous. Famous," she muttered. "He's making more money than he ever has. At least it looks like it."

"Good for him," I noted.

Both of us took a drink.

"You've been nice enough not to ask about Mayor Ryland, who, by the way, proposed to Polly." I had to get that little bit of gossip in. The look on Jolee's face was priceless. "I'm not upset about Finn taking over. It's probably a good thing. What I'm mad at is that he thinks I was going to hide the evidence against Mama."

There was no reason to tell Jolee about Mundy and my real reason for wanting to come shopping. Mama was no longer a suspect in my eyes, but the more I kept under wraps the better.

"I don't know what evidence you have against her. Why would he think that?" she asked, curling her hands around her mug.

"I taped my conversation with Camille the night of the murder. Some of the evidence points directly at Mama. Frank Von Lee was in the middle of writing his review of Mama's pot pie." I eased back in my chair. "Camille had gotten sick and excused herself to the bathroom. While she was gone I was talking to myself." Jolee looked at me like I was crazy. She'd really think I was a nut job if I told her I was talking to a ghost. "It helps me sort things out in my head to talk out loud. And on the tape I'd mentioned to myself that maybe I should hold on to the evidence until I got Mama a good lawyer."

"You said it out loud?" Her mouth dropped, and her brows creased. "That's stupid."

I could always count on Jolee to be real with me. That was one of the qualities I loved about her.

"Yeah. Well, Camille was so upset about Frank dying that I had Finn go to her office and get her official statement. Long story short..." I held the cup of coffee up to my chin and blew on it before I took a sip. "When we were listening to her statement, the little bit of me talking to myself was on there and I'd forgotten about it."

"And..." She leaned forward.

"And he thinks that morally I've compromised my legal authority, even though I didn't actually do it. I logged the information, I went to talk to Mama, I followed all protocol. Everything found in Frank's room that night pointed to Mama as his killer. You and I both know that she'd take much more pleasure in publicly humiliating Frank than in killing him." I chewed on the inside of my cheek waiting for Jolee's reply.

"Let me get this straight." She sat back. "Though you didn't do anything against your job, Finn is holding this against you morally?"

"We're getting together tonight, but it's kinda a cop thing when your morals are compromised." I shrugged.

"So now that you had nothing to do today, you called me to go shopping?" She was trying to figure out my ulterior motive.

"I shouldn't tell you this, but I'm going to keep investigating." I pointed to the outside. I guessed it was time to come clean. If I couldn't trust my best friend, who could I trust?

"I knew you were coming here and I need to go to Le Fork to get some information about Chef Mundy."

"What about him?" she asked.

"I'm not so sure he didn't set Mama up. In fact, he'd have all the reason to. He knew Frank from culinary school. Frank didn't pass him." I stopped talking when I noticed Jolee's surprised look. "What?"

"It's a big deal not to pass. I should know." She'd gone to culinary school, and she didn't need to remind me how she'd thought Ben was going to offer her a job but didn't. "But what does he have to do with Le Fork?"

"He'd been working there up until four weeks ago. That's when the Culinary Channel announced Frank Von Lee was going to come to Cottonwood." I drank the last bit of coffee in my cup.

"It was about four weeks ago that Ben talked to him. He'd even met with him a couple of times." Her jaw dropped. "Mundy did mention something about the pot pie too. He said that he'd love to have your mama's recipe if it was that good."

"In his room at the Tattered Cover Books and Inn, I found several attempted recipes for Mama's pot pie." I stared at her for a moment, knowing I shouldn't let her in on any more information about the case. But in for a penny, in for a pound. "Frank Von Lee was poisoned. There was a pot pie on his desk and an empty glass. One of them contained sodium fluoroacetate."

"What's that?" she asked, curling her nose.

"It's a fancy term for a poison that has all the side effects Camille reported Frank had before his heart attack. And I want to go see if they know anything over at Le Fork. I want Mundy's address too." I ran the pad of my finger around the edge of my empty cup.

"Then what are we waiting for?" Jolee stood up. "Let's go. I can help."

I smiled. Poppa ghosted into the shop.

"Great!" He bounced. "I knew she'd help you out."

I gulped, trying to stay focused on her.

"I was just over at Le Fork. They're hosting one of their cooking classes. Maybe one of you can distract them while someone goes into the office to take a look at the files." Poppa had a plan. "I found the employee files in the filing cabinet to the right of the desk. There are rows of filing cabinets that look like a bunch of recipes and orders."

This was information I could use.

"The files look to be alphabetized." Poppa looked disappointed. "I'm sorry I can't just open them and go through them for you. Somethings I can do. Somethings I can't." He held his hands in the air. "Still trying to figure all my new talents out. But have her take some photos with her phone." Poppa disappeared.

"I swear." Jolee stepped into the space where Poppa had just been. "Sometimes I think you've lost your mind."

"What?" I asked.

"I was talking to you and you were staring at me with a blank look on your face. You've been doing that a lot lately." She put her hands on her hips and narrowed her eyes.

"I've got a lot on my mind." I walked past her and out the

door. "I was thinking about the office in Le Fork. If they've got a class going, you can take the class and I can look around while you distract them."

"I can't take the class. I know too much." She did have a valid point.

"Okay." We walked through the parking lot, dodging moving cars as we made our way over to Le Fork. "I'll do the class. I need you to listen to me."

She nodded quickly. "This is exciting."

"Focus." I used two fingers, pointing to her eyes and then back to mine. "There's an office in the back. You need to find the employee files that are probably closest to the desk. There are going to be more filing cabinets in the office, but those are going to be invoices, recipes, and other things that we don't need."

She continued to drag her chin up and down. "The files next to the desk."

"Most times the employee files are alphabetized. When you find Mundy's file, don't worry about reading through it. I want you to take your phone and take pictures of every page that you can." I smiled to give her some confidence because there was a hint of reservation on her face. "You can do this."

"Yes. I can." She gave herself her own little pep talk before she walked into the shop and everyone looked at her.

"But don't bring attention to yourself," I muttered, knowing she'd just blown her cover.

Chapter Twenty

"Today we are discussing how to prepare a cake properly." The instructor stood in front of the baking class.

It'd cost me forty dollars to sign up and another sixty to purchase the items I needed to finish the three-course project of learning how to bake a cake. Fortunately for me, I had no idea how to bake a cake, so this was actually interesting to me and took my mind off of Jolee walking around snooping and waiting for the right opportunity to sneak into the back office.

"If you don't mind opening your book to page one, today we'll be going over different pans and different types of icing as well as the icing bags." The instructor went down the row of baking accessories on the table in front of her. "I'll teach you how to attach the tips and couplers to the bags so you can successfully pipe the icing on your cake."

You learn something new every day. I had no idea what those thingies were called. Couplers. I picked up a couple of them and noticed they were different sizes.

The first thing she had us do was mix the cake.

"It's very important that your oven is preheated for at least ten minutes," she said and had each of us preheat the oven we were using.

For the next five minutes she had us beat four eggs, then we added sugar and two teaspoons of vanilla extract. Sifting the dry ingredients was harder than I'd anticipated. Once we added it to the wet ingredients she had us use the whisk as we added milk and butter.

"You are doing a good job." Poppa stood next to me, looking into my bowl of batter. "How do you think Jolee is doing?"

"Jolee," I gasped. I'd completely lost track of time and Jolee.

I looked around and she was standing outside waving her phone at me.

"Are you going to put the batter in the pans?" The instructor had walked over when she noticed I'd become distracted. "You'll need two pans. The batter makes two cakes. Fill each of them halfway. After you do that, you will bake them for about twenty minutes."

"Oh, okay." I picked up the bowl and added the batter to each pan like she'd instructed.

Jolee ran into the room. "What are you doing?" she whispered, leaning her face into mine. "I've got the information. Let's go."

"What about my cakes?" I asked.

"Seriously?" Her eyes popped open, and her mouth fell. "I can bake you a cake." She put the tip of her finger in my batter and stuck it in her mouth before I could bat it away. "Mmm." Her lips flattened together. "Not bad. But I have a better tasting trick." She tugged on my arm. "Let's go."

"But I have twenty minutes and I paid for the class." I was surprised how much I enjoyed the class.

"I've got the information you wanted about you-know-who." She gave me a flat look.

"Another twenty minutes isn't going to clear Mama any quicker nor bring Frank back to the living." I opened the oven and put my two pans in side by side.

"I'm going to get the car." She held her hands out for my keys.

"Fine." I took the towel off my shoulder that I'd been using to clean up batter and threw it on my counter space. "You're going to teach me how to bake a cake?"

"Swear." She criss-crossed her finger over her heart. "Let's go."

I took one last look in the oven at my cakes before I followed out behind her.

"I really enjoyed that," I said once we got back in the Jeep.

"Fine." She huffed. "I got the information you wanted and I guess it's not going anywhere. So I'll go back to the boutique and buy my clothes and you go back and finish your cakes."

It sounded like a plan to me. It'd actually taken my mind off the investigation, but not for long. When I went back to my workstation, no one seemed to have noticed that I'd left. No one except for Poppa. His big nose was stuck in everyone else's batter.

"This just takes the cake," Poppa boasted. "Literally. You're a sheriff, not a baker."

I busied myself by checking the timer, flipping the oven light on and off to see my two cakes, and reading through the manual I'd paid a mint for.

"You're supposed to be trying to get your mama off the hook, not learning how to bake her a cake you can put a file in when she goes to jail." Poppa fumed in front of me.

I shooed him off and jerked the oven door open when the buzzer dinged.

The instructor walked over. She looked at the stick and peel nametag they'd given us. She bent down and looked into the oven.

"Kenni, those look nice and golden on top." Joy bubbled on her face and shone in her eyes. "Class," she smacked her hands together. "I love when a student pays attention. Look at Kenni's cakes. They're a nice golden brown and cooked throughout." She took a toothpick from my workstation and stuck it in the middle.

"If it wasn't cooked, there would be some soggy batter on the toothpick."

Other class participants' timers dinged and they were busy checking their cakes.

"Everyone will put their finished cakes on the cake rake. They need to cool for ten minutes." She looked at her watch. "Our time is up for today. I'll see you back here tomorrow where we're going to learn some basic decorating tips."

"Finally." Poppa did a little jig. "Let's get back to Cottonwood where we can help your mama."

Jolee had the Wagoneer pulled up to the curb. I motioned for her to scoot over to the passenger side.

"I enjoyed spying." Jolee rubbed her hands together vigorously. "It was so dangerous."

"Dangerous?" I jerked my head to look at her.

"Well, no, not really, but my adrenaline was running high. It was great," she squealed. "I can see why you love it so much."

I pulled out of the mall parking lot and headed back out of town toward Cottonwood.

"Don't get used to it. This was the only time I'll let you do it. And you can't tell anyone." I pointed my finger at her. "Not even Ben."

"I took some great photos of Mundy's file." She pulled her phone out of her purse. "Here's what they say." She used her finger to swipe the photos.

"Did you get his address?" I asked, knowing that I was going to make an unannounced visit.

"I got that, but the most interesting thing was his background check." She swiped her fingers apart on the screen making the photo bigger. "He was arrested a few years ago for disturbing the peace at the Culinary Institute in New York City. He was arrested in a class where the professor, Frank Von Lee, had used some sort of egg that was endangered. Apparently

Mundy is an environmentalist and protested."

"Not much of one since he slaughtered the chicken for the pot pie recipe." I thought about how I could get my hands on Frank Von Lee's class list. It wasn't like I could tell Finn to get one and check out the others in the class.

"I didn't say he wasn't a meat eater, just an environmentalist." Jolee spent the next few minutes scrolling through the phone. "Here is his last known address."

She read it off to me. I wasn't familiar with the area.

"Can you text me the photos?" I asked.

"Sure will." Jolee tapped, swiped, and punched on the phone. A few seconds later my phone chirped with texts one after the other. "There ya go. What's next?"

"I'm going to drop you off at the office and I've got to go to my parents'. I told my mama I'd come for supper. After that, Finn is stopping by for a drink." The Jeep rattled back across the Cottonwood county line. I was really excited for the late-night cocktail. "Have you heard of any sort of Botox ring going around?"

"Kenni, you make it sound like some drug ring." Jolee laughed. She stopped when she saw I wasn't joking.

"Have you seen my mama?" I asked. "Her face is so botched up from a Botox party that I'm not even sure if it's going to go back to normal."

"So she didn't get the black eye from Frank?" Jolee asked.

"You heard she and Frank got into a fight?" I asked.

"You know Cottonwood," she said. "Anyways, you have to be invited to one of those parties, and from what I hear they don't give you much notice."

"If you get invited, will you call me?" I asked.

"Sure. I think Katy Lee had an invite from someone that she sold insurance to. I'll check into it." Her words were music to my ears.

I could get at least one case solved while Finn worked on Mama's. Well, Frank's. I couldn't help but wonder what Finn was doing differently than I'd done. It'd be interesting to see.

I slowed down the Wagoneer when we got into the city limits. In no time we'd gone through the three stoplights in town and turned down the alley behind the department.

Jolee checked her phone.

"We made it back just in time for me to go get the Meals on Wheels." She put her hand on the handle of the door. "Listen, I know that you aren't going back to the office." Her eyes shifted out the window and towards the office door. "I know that if I follow you, which I won't, you're going to go find Mundy."

"What if I am?" I asked.

"Then I'd tell you to be careful." She reached over and we hugged. "I've got a newfound respect for your job since I went undercover." She winked and got out of the car.

"Actually, I only have a few minutes before I told Mama I'd be there. So I'm going to head down to the library and look a little bit more into Frank Von Lee's background. Maybe something will jump out at me." I waved bye and she shut the door.

Before I went into the library I called Finn.

"How's it going?" I asked.

"You know. People calling all day about the investigation. Betty ran Mundy's background," he said. "I went to his house to see him. He said he knew Frank from school but no way did he kill him. He said that he didn't know that Frank was even coming to Ben's when he called Ben for a job."

Right. Liar, I thought.

"Anyways, I'm going to do more digging on him. He's a strange dude," Finn said.

"Are we still on for tonight?" I asked.

"Yes, we are. I can't wait. See you soon." With that we hung up.

Cottonwood's library was located in a small white colonial-style building next to the courthouse. Parking was on the street. The inside of the library smelled exactly as if I'd just opened up a book and stuck my nose inside. That paper smell was always a welcomed scent and brought back fond memories of me getting lost in my fictional worlds when I was a kid and Mama was at her church meetings. Maybe I'd take up more reading since all this time fell into my hands.

There were three rooms to the library: the children's room, the fiction room, and the non-fiction room. It wasn't like they were stuck in the olden times. They had a couple of computers and everything that'd been on microfiche had been digitized into the computer system. That included articles of major magazines. I hoped I could find something, anything on Frank Von Lee.

"Good afternoon, almost evening," Marcy Carver greeted me from behind the reference desk as soon as I walked in. "What are you looking for, Kenni?"

Marcy never aged. It was probably from working in a nice quiet place with no stress, but still, she'd always had the same hairstyle—I'd never seen her without her hair pulled up in a thick top knot on her head. Once I'd asked her about her hair and she told me that if she didn't pull it back, her hair would spring out all over the place. Her dark skin was smooth milk chocolate and her brown eyes were just as lovely as her.

"I've come to get some information on Frank Von Lee." I leaned on the counter. "But tell me, how's your family?"

"Oh, you know. Wade had them grandkids over for the weekend. They wore me out. I was never so happy to get back to the library." She blinked and then focused her eyes on me. "But I've beat you to the punch." She walked over to her desk and picked up a stack of papers and magazines. "I too was curious about our visiting celebrity."

She pushed the pile across the counter.

"Edna Easterly came in here earlier today looking for some articles too, but I knew she'd use them in the Chronicle and I'm a little sore at her for printing that picture of your mama. She knows better, so I didn't give this to her." She cocked her right brow. "She's going to have to go to the city to find any information on him."

"You are a true friend." I reached over the counter and patted her on the arm. "Do you mind if I take these back there and read over them?"

"Not at all." She winked.

I picked up the stack and headed over to one of the empty tables with a computer on it. Marcy had already organized the stack starting with the beginning of Frank Von Lee's career and continuing up until a few weeks ago when it announced he'd made his decision to visit Cottonwood.

There were several articles about his class and how prestigious it was to be accepted into it. There was only one mention of Mundy, and it was just a class roster that accompanied a photo of the seven students Frank had accepted into the class that year.

I typed the year of the class into the computer along with Mundy's name as a search tag and a link to a court document came up. I pulled my phone out and scrolled through the photos Jolee had sent me. The court document on the computer matched the court papers in his file. With a few clicks, I logged into the Kentucky police database that was tied into the national law-enforcement database. With Mundy's social security number from the file, I was able to plug that into the database and see that Mundy's record was clean other than the arrest.

I scrolled through the court papers on the police database. It looked like Mundy was kicked out of the class because he had lashed out at Frank. Instead of Frank Von Lee pressing charges for Mundy's assault, Frank took out a restraining order against Mundy. An order was re-filed just a couple of weeks ago for a court date in a month.

"What the hell is that all about?" I whispered, scrolling down a little more to see if there'd been a reason listed for the re-file. "Oh, Mundy, how you lie."

There was no reason listed, but I knew that restraining orders were only re-filed if there was a direct threat. With Frank dead, there was sure a direct threat on his life. I knew this was more incriminating that anything Mama did.

I hit the print button and the printer next to the computer going off was music to my ears. While I waited for it to finish, I wondered about the other people in the class. They'd been witnesses to any sort of disagreement between Mundy and Frank.

Using the mouse, I clicked on the history button on the screen and scrolled to where I'd seen the class list. I double clicked and brought that page back up. I printed it too.

After I made sure the printer had printed the papers I wanted, I clicked out of the computer and made sure I cleared the history so no one could go back through and see what I was looking at, though they'd need my passwords. You could never be too careful.

This was some great evidence that pointed to a tiff between the victim and Mundy that had to be looked into. Was it revenge? I'd think a restraining order wasn't good for a chef's reputation, especially from a famous food critic. But more importantly, I felt like this was the solid evidence to clear Mama as the number one suspect.

The more I dug, the more I read about how Frank Von Lee had really done a number on people's lives. He really wasn't a very nice man, but it still didn't warrant someone killing him. Frank Von Lee either made you rich or poor. Nothing in between. If he came to your restaurant and gave you a great review, you'd made it in the restaurant business. On the other hand, if you got a bad review, from what I read, most of the restaurants went bankrupt. Frank had even been sued by a family by the name of Tooke. It was a big case that was eventually dropped after the owner committed suicide.

My phone rang.

"Mama," I groaned, noticing the little digital time on my phone said I was late.

"Kenni, can you please come over right now?" She sounded desperate.

"Right now?" I asked in my hushed library voice. "Why?"

"I really need you to come now. I don't want to say it over the phone." There was an urgency in her voice that really bothered me.

"I'm on my way," I said and gathered up the papers. I hung up the phone and stuck it back in my pocket as I made my way to the exit. "Thanks, Marcy. You're a gem."

I put her file back on the counter and headed on out of the door.

Downtown Cottonwood had a yawning peace as the late afternoon dragged into the early evening. It was the time of day when everyone had left work to make it home in time for supper and every shop in town closed for the night, except for Ben's, probably where Finn and I would end up later tonight.

The diner was still hopping. I slowed the Jeep down and noticed through the windows of the diner all the tables were filled and Ben was busy taking orders. It looked like his fears had not come to fruition and that made me happy. Soon he and Jolee would be back to normal. Hopefully the case would be solved and peace would return to our small southern town.

I pushed the gas and headed on back down Main Street and turned right on Free Row. Duke had been home and it wasn't fair of me to leave him there when he loved going to my parents' house.

"Let's go, Duke!" I yelled after I opened the door to the house. His back legs flung out from under him when he took the turn at the door too fast, skidding outside. "You're my crazy dog."

He jumped and yelped at the gate, waiting for me to walk over.

"Let's go," I teased my already anxious pup when I opened the gate.

"Hi, Kenni." Mrs. Brown waved from her front porch. Riley Titan was screwing a light bulb in her outside porch lamp. "Have you met Riley? He's very handy."

"Hi, Riley." I greeted them when I walked over. "Yes, Mrs. Brown, I've met Riley."

"Mrs. Brown heard all the banging I'm doing over at Deputy Vincent's house and she asked me to come by and look at her light." He held up the bulb. "Just a bulb out. Easy fix."

"It wasn't the banging that got my attention. It was the yelling." Mrs. Brown's chin dipped.

"Yelling?" I questioned.

"It's nothing." Riley played it off.

"Nothing, my patookie," Mrs. Brown said sternly. "Danny Shane has lost his mind."

"Oh, really. It's no big deal. I'm used to big companies and bullying." Riley shook off Mrs. Brown's comments. "He heard I'd gotten the job offer from Deputy Vincent and he came to bust my chops. It wasn't a big deal."

"It was a big deal," Mrs. Brown protested. "He was going to slug you. Then he saw my wooden rolling pin." She nodded with pride.

"Rolling pin?" I half laughed. Mrs. Brown swinging around a rolling pin was something I'd like to have seen.

"You should've seen her come to my rescue." Riley smiled. Mrs. Brown was smitten with him.

"You didn't need no rescue." Mrs. Brown winked.

"If y'all excuse me. I better get back to work before Deputy Vincent gets home and fires me." Riley waved on his way back down to Finn's house.

"That's strange about Danny," I said. He'd always been a little hotheaded, but he wasn't a bully or a thug. It made me wonder what was going on with him. Maybe a little friendly visit to Danny Shane was on the docket.

Then my mind did that thing. It went to the what-ifs. Not that any evidence pointed to Danny, but what if he was so mad at Ben for losing the job that his revenge was to shut down Ben's? After all, he did say that Ben's had given him food poisoning and he told everyone he knew not to go there. Malina did say that Danny had been at The Tattered Cover Books and Inn for a couple of days fixing things up.

"That's it." I ran my hand down Duke once we said goodbye to Mrs. Brown. "Danny Shane hasn't showed up for jobs. What's going on with him?" I whispered on the way to the Jeep. "Plus he owns those condos where Mama said she got her Botox. Maybe it's time I start investigating that."

Chapter Twenty-One

"What do you think your mama wants?" Poppa sat in the front seat and Duke jumped into the back.

"You and I both know that she's got something up her sleeve. I hope she doesn't have a bomb she wants to drop on me about the Botox and stuff. Regardless, I think we need to go see Danny Shane tomorrow before I go back to my baking class."

"I'm not convinced Danny Shane is a murderer, but he'll do anything to keep that family business going. His dad was just like him," Poppa said.

"I'm not saying he's a murderer, I'm just saying he might know more than he's leading on." I continued, "I can just make a courtesy call to him and see what my gut says after I talk to him."

"Remember to always listen to your gut." Poppa ghosted away as I pulled up to my parents' house.

"You are going to have to stay with Mrs. Brown all day tomorrow," I said to Duke. "I've got some investigating to do."

Some familiar cars were lined up on the street. Ones that belonged to Tibbie Bell, Myrna Savage, Viola White, Ruby Smith, Missy Jennings, and the On The Run food truck, which meant that Jolee was there. If it weren't the wrong night, I'd think the Euchre girl's night in was tonight since it was the same gals that played.

The sun was setting and it was getting darker as well as colder. All of the lights were on in Mama's house. I dragged my old sweatshirt out of the back and tugged it on.

"What on earth is she up to?" I asked Duke. I swear he understood me. "Come on, boy." I patted my leg and walked up to the door.

When I opened it, laughter and chatter filtered into the entryway.

"There you are," Mama greeted me with joy. "I thought I heard a car door."

It was a far cry from her attitude since I'd last seen her. She even had her black eye covered with makeup. Though she was still a little puffy, she looked a whole lot better.

"What's going on?" I dragged my hand along Duke as he ran past me into Mama's house.

"I thought that after last night's horrible town council meeting, we'd move our weekly Euchre game up to today. You love Euchre and I think you need a bit of cheering up." She twirled on her gold flats and trotted into the other room.

I wasn't sure if Mama used the excuse to cheer herself up or if she really was trying to cheer me up. Either way, I was glad to get out of my head for a few hours. And the food wouldn't be bad either.

Every week all the girls got together for our Euchre night. Everyone brought a dish, and not just any dish. It was the best they'd make all week. These women took pride in their cooking and if they could outdo each other, they'd do it.

By the sound of my gurgling stomach, tonight was not going to disappoint. Mama's kitchen table was filled with all the southern appetizers.

"Myrna, is this your spicy pimento cheese?" I asked.

I could already taste Myrna's specialty appetizer. I used the fancy spoon in the cheese spread to put some on a couple of toast points.

"Don't forget the asparagus." She grinned. I noticed the

wrinkles in her smile line were smooth.

"You look good." I took the tongs and placed a piece of asparagus on top of the pimento cheese. "Are you using a different moisturizer?" I baited her. "This winter my skin took a hit. I've been looking in the beauty aisle at Dixon's for something new."

She licked her lips and hesitated. "You really think I look good?"

"Yes." I nodded.

Come on, Myrna, I thought, tell me about the Botox.

"Or did you get it from Tiny Tina's? I know she's got a new cosmetics line down there." I reached over and put a few fried dill pickles on my plate.

"Well," she leaned into my shoulder and whispered, "there's this new party, kinda like the one that Katy Lee has with that clothing line." She reached over me and took a couple of the shrimp and grits.

"Shabby Trends?" I asked, pretending I didn't know.

"It's not clothes. It's Botox." She smiled and pointed to her lips. "Your mama and I went to get a little for only twenty-five dollars. She had a little reaction, but I didn't." She rolled her eyes Mama's way.

"I saw that she had that black eye." I pretended Mama hadn't said a word to me. "Of course, Edna printed it on the front page of the Chronicle so everyone would assume she and Frank Von Lee had an argument."

"Wasn't that a shame?" Myrna tsked. "Your mama wasn't there when he died, so I don't know why they think she was."

"Myrna, do you know something?" I asked. "It doesn't look good for Mama, and if you do have some information I'd like to know it. Any information can be helpful even if you don't think it could be."

"Your mama was pitching a fit after her eye swelled up and

blackened. She was going to go back over there and give them a piece of her mind. Alone," she muttered uneasily. "I told her that there's no way I was going to let her go alone. You know those condos are a little fishy. We went and she demanded her money back. They told her since it was cash only, they didn't offer money back. Then she said that her daughter was the sheriff and she was going to report them. That's when they got a little antsy."

"They did?" I drew back and acted like it was no big deal they were there.

"Her threats worked. They gave her money back and told her to come back and they'd fix the botch." Myrna laughed. "Leave it to your mama to get a bad batch of Botox. Especially when she needed it for Frank Von Lee. Bless her heart." Myrna lovingly glanced at Mama, who was on the other side of the room talking. "Nothing has gone right for her with this Frank thingy. First she wears herself out cooking to make sure each pot pie tastes the same as the next. Then she goes and gets Botox so she can look good, only it's all messed up. Then Poor Frank up and gets himself killed. Poor shame."

"It sure is. Say, do you know the number of the apartment?" I asked.

So as not to seem so interested, I continued to put more food on my plate.

"I thought you'd never ask." She grinned. "You could stand to get those elevens done."

"Elevens?" Never in a million years did I think Myrna Savage would give me beauty tricks.

"These two lines you have between your eyes." She reached up and touched the top of my nose. "They look like an eleven. I had one." She dragged her nail between her brows. "It might cost a little more, but you'll look a lot better. Or," she let out an audible sigh, "you could get bangs. That'd do it too."

"Elevens. Good to know. Thanks." I nodded. "What's the apartment number?"

"Twenty-two. Two, two. Twenty-two." She made sure I remembered. "Tell 'em I sent ya. Maybe they'll give me a discount next time."

"Twenty-two. Got it." I reached over the Crock-Pot. "Y'all have outdone yourselves. Are these Dr. Pepper meatballs?"

"They sure are." Pride showed on her face. She smiled, line-free.

With my plate full and a Diet Coke in my hand, I made my way into Mama's fancy family room where she'd set up the Euchre tables.

Jolee, my partner, was sitting with Ruby Smith and Viola White.

"Any news about you-know-who?" Jolee asked about Mundy.

"No," I said and shuffled the cards, dealing them out to the four of us and waiting to see if any of them wanted me to pick up the red nine on top of the discarded pile of cards.

Each of them knocked their finger on the table. In Euchre talk, they were passing on the nine. I flipped it over and now they had the opportunity to call a trump suit. Each of them passed, but not me. I never passed when I could call a trump, even if I didn't have the highest cards.

"Spades is trump," I called the suit.

For the next half hour, everyone made chitchat without mentioning Frank Von Lee or Mama's involvement. No one made mention of Mama's face or the awful photo Edna had printed. They didn't even mention the Culinary Channel at all.

Until...

"I'm tired of everyone beating around the bush." Viola White's eyes gazed over the top of her cards that she held up in front of her face. She'd opted for a cream turban with her hair tucked up underneath. A necklace with large gold balls the size of eggs wrapped around her neck.

Viola was a substitute. She didn't have a regular partner and tonight she was Ruby Smith's partner. Both old. Both wealthy.

I sucked in a deep breath, waiting for what Viola was going to say and if Mama would end up kicking her out. I threw down the jack of spades, the highest of the round we were playing, hoping to pull out more trump cards. Viola threw a nine of hearts, which told me she had no trump in her hand, while Jolee dropped the queen of spades. Ruby's eyes went back and forth between her cards and the cards played before she finally gave up the jack of clubs, the second highest card in the round.

"And what would that be, Viola?" I asked.

"What on earth do y'all think about Polly Parker marrying Mayor Ryland?" Ruby arranged her cards and rearranged them again.

"Money, honey. Chance Ryland has a boatload." Viola's mouth quirked with humor.

She seemed to have a deep secret about the mayor and his wealth. Of course I couldn't help but wonder what that was.

"If I were Pete Parker, I'd take that girl and give her a good whoopin'. I just can't hold my tongue no more." Viola dragged her long nails down the black feather boa wrapped around her neck, her turquoise rings really standing out against the black. "I know you really like the Parkers, Ruby, but that's ridiculous."

Relief swam through my veins and I eased back in my seat, thankful they didn't bring up Frank, Mama, or me being taken off the case.

"I agree." Ruby took the break to pull out her lipstick and circle her lips with the bright orange color. "There are plenty of women his own age to do that to than that poor girl."

"I can't even imagine what she sees in his wrinkly body,"

Jolee threw in her two cents.

There was a collective snicker around the table.

"Can you imagine in a few years when her boobs'll still be all perky and up here," Viola flattened her hands under her chin, "and she's pushing him in a wheelchair?"

"Or worse," Ruby's eyes shifted side to side with an evil grin on her face, "her visiting him along with her mama and daddy in a nursing home."

The two women laughed and cackled as I threw more cards, ending the first game in our Euchre round, giving me and Jolee the first win in the set.

"He is very mature looking." I thought it was time to give a little positive spin to it. "She's going to need a caterer." I rose a brow toward Jolee.

She looked at me, but in a through-me kind of way.

"Hmm." Her lips twisted. "That's an idea." The thought brought a smile to her face.

"She works for you, so she's going to need jewelry." I threw the conversation toward Viola White. "You know her wedding will be in all the social papers."

They all knew that when you made it into the societal page of the Chronicle, you were Cottonwood royalty.

"Remember when Tiny Tina's was mentioned in there after that celebrity passed through and stopped to get a quick massage," I said. "She was booked for two years after that."

"You might be onto something." Ruby tapped the edge of her card on the table in front of her before she threw it in the middle to take the next trump. "I wonder if she's going to have an outdoor wedding because I have all those cute chandeliers that can be repurposed into romantic hanging lighting. It's in all the wedding magazines."

"It's settled then." I threw down a trump to get the game finished. They followed suit. "Viola will host an engagement party for Polly. Jolee will do the food. Ruby can bring her chandelier idea. We'll make Polly think it's her idea as we present them to her."

"You're a genius." Ruby reached over and patted my hand. "You are a great sheriff."

"All joking aside," Viola drummed her nails on the table, "I'm not happy Mayor Ryland took you off the case without a full council vote."

"Unfortunately, the law does state that the mayor can govern over the department if there's a conflict." I raked in all the cards and handed them to Jolee so she could shuffle and deal.

"Regardless," Ruby chimed in, "all of us are here for you and if you need anything, you know we'll drop whatever we're doing."

Jolee smiled at me from across the table.

"I'll keep that in mind." I smiled back.

"You know," Jolee shuffled the cards into a bridge, "our sheriff is a mighty good baker. In fact, she's been taking a baking class."

"You never know. I might be trying to get a job down at the bakery if I'm out of work soon," I joked.

"Are you baking a cake for a certain someone?" Ruby asked.

"Oh, spill. How does Finn feel about you not taking lead on the case?" Viola followed up.

"First off, no. I'm learning to bake for me. Secondly, Finn and I both want what's best for Cottonwood." I had to be very political.

"Are you two being nosy?" Mama walked up behind me and put her hands on my shoulders. "I, for one, am thrilled to have this extra time with my baby."

"Me too, Mama." I reached up and patted her on the hand. "Me too."

As much as Mama drove me crazy, I knew she always had my back. Even though she'd rather go to jail over a murder charge than have people find out she had Botox, I was going to have her back. Maybe it was time to get the elevens done.

Chapter Twenty-Two

It was actually a very nice day, I thought to myself on my way back to the house. It was the first time in a long time that I'd actually taken a few hours to enjoy myself. Even though I wasn't a big shopper, the laughter and storytelling going on between me and Jolee was a lot of fun and the surprise Euchre game mama had thrown together was also enjoyable.

But tonight when Finn stopped by, now that was something I was really looking forward to. Only there was one thing on my list that had to be done: calling the people on Mundy's class list. If I really wanted to give Finn some solid evidence about why I thought Mundy killed Frank, then I needed some eyewitnesses to Frank and Mundy's volatile relationship.

"Boo," Poppa teased as he appeared in the kitchen.

Duke jumped up at the ready to play toss with him. I'd just grabbed a beer and retrieved the papers I'd printed off from the library with Frank's class list.

"What are those?" Poppa asked.

"Names of the students in Frank Von Lee's class." I sat down in a kitchen chair and tapped the papers. "Mundy was in this class."

"He was?" Poppa's ghost somehow kicked the ball Duke had dropped at his feet and Duke shot off down the hall. "That's a connection."

"I found it today." I looked up at him. It started to feel like old times.

At this very table when I was a teenager and even in the academy, Poppa and I use to banter back and forth about his cases. It was something I loved to do.

"Mundy not only got kicked out of Frank's class, Frank had a restraining order against him. Just a few weeks ago, the restraining order was re-filed, which means that Frank had reason to keep Mundy a good distance from him."

"I hope you're going to go and confront Mundy, because if Frank was to show up at the diner and Mundy was there, he'd be in violation of the order." Poppa raised a good point.

"I really don't think it's a coincidence that Mundy called Ben to see if Ben needed help." I recalled how Ben told me that he'd been searching for a chef to help out so he could focus his time on Frank's visit.

"It wasn't like it was a big secret that Frank was coming." Poppa looked over my shoulder and at the paper. "I guess you better use that fancy laptop of yours to look these people up. If we can get even two of them to confirm the tension between teacher and student, it's enough evidence to make Mundy a suspect."

"The restraining order is enough." I dragged my laptop in front of me. I took a big swig of my beer before I got started.

I used the police database to see if any of them had criminal records. It wasn't unusual for chefs to get into some sort of fight in their career and get arrested for something really stupid. Poppa had arrested Ben once. There was a customer who complained and insulted his food. Ben didn't take the criticism very well, and the customer called the sheriff's department. Poppa didn't have a choice but to put Ben in the pokey for a few hours until he calmed down.

"I'm hoping the restraining order wasn't just because Mundy lost his cool." It did tickle my brain that Frank Von Lee would use something so silly to put a restraining order on

Mundy, though it did help Mama's case.

With a few keystrokes, I found a couple of the people on Facebook. They were a little older than in their class photo, but it was definitely them. I clicked on the messenger tab and viola. Their phone numbers were right there. "That was easy. Thank goodness for social media."

"Huh?" Poppa's eyes narrowed.

"This is like email." I pointed to the blue messenger box. "Some people actually put their phone numbers in their profile and anyone can call them. This guy," I pointed to the profile photo, "he's this guy." I pointed to the younger version of him in the class photo I'd printed at the library. "And his profile says he's a chef."

"There weren't very many people in the class." Poppa bent down and looked at the class photo.

"It's some sort of exclusive, prestigious class. So Mundy must be good as a chef," I said and typed in the phone number. "Hello, is this Guy Hall?" I questioned when someone answered.

When he confirmed, I continued, "My name is Kenni Lowry. I'm the Sheriff in Cottonwood, Kentucky."

"You mean where Chef Von Lee was killed?" he questioned from the other end of the phone.

"Yes. And we are going through Frank, er, Chef Von Lee's students and we've come across someone you might know from your class."

"You're talking about Mundy, right? What a tool." There was obviously no love lost between them.

"I see that Mundy made an impression on you too."

Duke jumped up from underneath my feet and ran to the back door. Finn was there and waved at me through the screen door. I waved him in.

"He made that impression on everyone," Guy said.

I put my finger up to my mouth when Finn walked in. He

had a brown sack with him.

"Dinner," he mouthed and sat it down on the kitchen table.

I pulled the phone away from my ear and pushed the speaker button so Finn could hear.

"Did you actually see any of the tension between Mundy and Frank?" I asked.

"Oh, yeah. Mundy was always telling Chef how he was doing things wrong. Chef was really good at ignoring him until Mundy got in his face about how to make country gravy of all things." Guy laughed.

"Country gravy?" I asked, making sure I'd heard right.

"Yeah. Mundy really thought he was this great southern chef. It wasn't until years later when Chef finally took out a restraining order on Mundy. I was there when it happened." Now he was giving me some good info.

"Where and when was this?" I asked and pushed all the papers I'd printed off from the library towards Finn to help clue him in on what was going on.

"I was taking Chef's master class and Mundy had scored a seat, which I don't know how that happened. Chef told us about the Culinary Channel and how they were giving him his own show about southern foods. Mundy went nuts and that's when the cops were called. The next class Chef told us that he had to put a restraining order on Mundy." There was a pause. Finn and I looked at each other. "Mundy literally went crazy, saying he was the best southern chef and it was a joke."

"Guy, thank you for answering my questions. If I have any more, can I call you back?" I asked with my finger on the end button.

"No problem. I'm more than happy to get that whacko behind bars." The line went dead.

"That was a bit of news." Finn pulled out Chinese containers from the bag.

"Today I went to the library and did a little digging." I gestured to the papers he'd looked over. "This for sure points to Mundy as the killer. Not only does he have a motive of jealousy, but there was a restraining order against him."

Finn looked over the papers and I grabbed a couple of plates and forks. There were some chopsticks, but I'd never learned to use them.

"Ms. Kim threw in some extra fortune cookies." He looked up at me and winked. "She said I was going to need as much good fortune as I could get."

I rolled my eyes. Mrs. Kim was the owner of Kim's Buffet and mother of my friend Gina. She acted like she didn't like me, but deep down I knew she did.

"With all this information, I'm definitely going to tell Mayor Ryland that Vivian Lowry is no longer a suspect. I know we already established that, but it's not official. I want to make it official." Finn scooted his chair next to mine and sat down. He put his arm around me. "I'll do a stakeout at Mundy's and drag him into the department for an interrogation tomorrow."

"That's perfect." I nuzzled my nose in his neck, sitting there in the comfort of his arms. Duke didn't let us sit there for too long before he came over and dropped a ball at Finn's feet.

"Ahem," There was a throat clearing from the corner. Without a shadow of a doubt, Finn was getting a little too close for Poppa's comfort.

Chapter Twenty-Three

The smell of freshly brewing coffee was the first thing that woke me up. The second thing that woke me up: Mama.

"Good morning, Mama," I answered the phone and looked at the time.

"You're still in bed?" Mama asked.

"It's my day off." Not that I really had a day off, but it was my usual day that I went in late to the office. After last night, I was certain Finn would get Mundy in the office, brought up on charges of murdering Frank Von Lee, and booked.

Though it was only a little past seven a.m., it was past my normal six a.m. wake-up time.

"Fiddle fart! Get up," Mama yelled. "We're celebrating."

I pulled the phone from my ear. Duke looked up from the foot of the bed and then slid his front paws off the edge, followed by his body. He pulled himself into a long stretch and let out a groan before he walked out of the room.

"Did you see the paper?" she asked.

"No. Why? What are we celebrating?" I wondered what'd happened.

"I'm no longer a suspect. Mayor Ryland said in an interview that there's another suspect in the case," she informed me.

"I'm up." I flung the covers off me and swung my feet over the edge. A shiver of cold rushed up through my feet. I pushed myself up to stand. "I can't celebrate. I've got some work to do." I padded my way down to the kitchen and pushed the back door open for Duke to run out to do his morning business.

"You just said that you were off today." She used my words against me. Since when did Mama listen to me? "So get up and let's go get your elevens done."

I put my finger up to my elevens.

"Myrna told you about our conversation?" I asked.

"Yep. And if you're going to arrest them, then I want to be there." Her voice escalated. "They ruined my face."

"You should've known better than to think legitimate Botox would only cost twenty-five dollars." I opened my cabinet and retrieved a coffee cup. "I appreciate all your enthusiasm to shut them down, but I can't drag you along. It's a sheriff's department matter. Don't go back over there. I can't just go in guns blazing. That's not how investigations work."

Though I wished sometimes that they did. Cutting through all the red tape felt like it took way too long at times.

"I really think you should take me. I can be your deputy on this one." Mama was serious. "Deputize me."

Two days ago she wanted me to cuff her and now she wanted me to deputize her. Mama never ceased to shock me.

"Not today, Mama." I wasn't about to put her in the middle of an investigation. "I'll give you a call later."

"But..." Mama faltered. "Grab your umbrella. Rain's a'comin'."

"Bye." I hung up the phone and walked over to let Duke in. "Rain, my hinny," I whispered and shut the door. There wasn't a call for rain in the forecast for a week or so.

I headed back down the hall and into my bedroom. There was no reason to hang around here any longer when I needed to get my day started. I had a to-do list that had Danny Shane's name right at the top. Even though we had good reason to believe Mundy was the killer, I still had unanswered questions about his behavior. Under his name on my list were the condos by the river to check out that Botox ring and then my baking class. Out of all of those things I was surprisingly most excited about the class.

Five minutes later, I'd gotten my shower and pulled on a t-shirt and jeans.

Poppa ghosted into my bedroom. "You need to get down to the department and do a timeline, not only to show that your mama didn't kill Frank, but one for Mundy."

"I'll do that after hours. I want to give Finn time to do his job and check Mundy out. So we are going to unofficially go see Danny Shane this morning." I pulled a sweatshirt out of my drawer and tugged on my cowboy boots. "After that, I've got to head to Le Fork for cake class."

"Cake class?" Poppa obviously didn't like that. "What about the condos? You need to get some kind of justice for your mama's face."

"That's on the list too," I assured him.

He disappeared. I was right behind him after I'd gotten Duke settled and called Mrs. Brown to remind her to check in on him throughout the day.

The sun had faded behind a cloud on my way to the Jeep. I stopped and looked up, giving the air a little sniff. Maybe Mama was right. There was a salty rain smell that was similar to the smell before a big gully washer. I almost walked back inside to grab my rain boots, but the sun peeked out, pushing Mama's observation aside. I was good at believing whatever came from Mama's mouth. She had a way of doing that.

I jumped in my Jeep and headed down Free Row toward the stop sign. The neighborhood was still asleep and all was calm for the time being. At the end of the street I took a left on Main Street going north to visit Danny Shane. The sun hid behind some really dark clouds. I flipped on WCKK just in time to hear the weather update that an unexpected rain shower had begun to move in on Cottonwood but was not expected to last long.

"Spring showers bring May flowers," I repeated Mama's mantra as little dots of sprinkles appeared on the windshield.

That wasn't going to dampen my mood. I couldn't help but smile seeing the line of customers waiting outside to get a seat at Ben's as I drove past. It was about time he did well, even if it was because of a murder. When I was stopped by the stoplight, I loved seeing the Cottonwood Chronicle headline that "Ben's Is Booming" along with a picture of Ben at the stove with a big smile on his face.

Shane's Construction had been around as long as I could remember. The Shane family ran the business and all three generations had been involved. I'd never ever had a complaint or even heard of any shoddy jobs completed by their company. Something else that I hadn't heard was that Danny had recently taken over the company like Ben had said.

Danny had always been the hardheaded one of his family. He was the only one who really stood up to the mayor and the council when he'd proposed to have the condos built on a plot of land overlooking the Kentucky River. The mayor wanted to keep Cottonwood small, which only hurt our economy where Danny saw the feature and the value of having condos on the river. It not only brought new residents to Cottonwood, but also a community of people who loved the river and started to invest for their retirement here, giving the economy a boost.

The condos where Mama had said she'd gone to get her bad Botox fix. Shane Construction not only built the condos, they still owned the complex plus the land and benefited from the Home Owners Association fee. The thought that he might know about the Botox parties crossed my mind too.

If he did, and if he really did have reason to get back at Ben, then Danny Shane wasn't in his right frame of mind.

"Sheriff." Danny greeted me at the door of the aluminum building that was a temporary office for the new concrete two-story building they'd recently gotten approval from the council to build. "This doesn't look like a personal visit."

He stepped out and greeted me halfway. The cowboy hat was pulled down on his forehead, making a shadow draw down his face. He had his red and black plaid shirt tucked into his tight blue jeans. The sun made his shadow look seven feet tall instead of his six-foot-six frame. A little intimidating.

The grey clouds blanketed the once unblemished grass of the family's three-hundred-acre dairy farm land. The sprinkle that'd fallen on the Jeep on Main Street had finally made its way out to the country. The dry dirt we were standing on would be a big old mud pile soon. Good for muddin' around on four wheelers. I couldn't help but think what Danny's grandfather would say about him digging up their farm and putting that concrete building on it.

His grandfather took pride in their cows. The dairy farm was still on the back one hundred acres and up and running. We were one of few counties that still had milk delivery. And it wasn't cheap to have that fresh milk delivered. Jolee said the cost was nothing compared to the taste that made her recipes so good.

"I've got a couple of questions for you." I slammed the back door of the Wagoneer.

"I'll try to answer them." He strolled a little closer, his boots crunching into the temporary gravel drive.

I glanced up at the sky when I felt a drop of rain. "Looks like a gully washer's coming."

"It'll be good for the crops." He dug his hands into his jean pockets and kept an eye on me.

"How's everything going, Danny?" I asked.

"Construction business has been so busy. It's hard to find

good help." He slid his eyes up to the darkening sky. "Do you want to come in out of the rain? I've got some coffee brewing."

"That'd be nice." I offered a smile.

Breaking bread was a great way to ease into a conversation and socialize. In this case coffee was going to have to do.

I headed into the barn, which might seem silly to some. Not around these parts. Most barns on working farms were nicer than the houses the farmers lived in. Same with Danny's. The floor was a nice poured concrete. The stalls were on the right and the offices were on the left. In Danny's case, he had his dairy and construction office in his barn while his employees were in the other building.

"Your mama and them doing all right?" Danny asked, offering the go-ahead to fix my own coffee from the coffee bar in his office.

I grabbed a Styrofoam cup and poured a hot cup of coffee.

"They're fine." I nodded, not sure what to say. "I guess you probably know I'm not here for pleasantries." I used a stirrer to add creamer to my coffee. "I wanted to know what's going on between you and Ben." I turned around to face him.

He was sitting in the chair behind his desk and gestured for me to sit down in the chair in front.

"That so-called job of Ben's was charity."

"Charity?" I asked and blew on the steaming coffee before I took a sip.

"Ben Harrison is having a hard time paying the bills. He came to me with a sad sack story about how he needed to update the restaurant to make it look good for TV. He said that if he won..." Danny shook his head. "He didn't even give credit to your mama." His eyes looked under his brows at me. "Anyways, he said if he won, then he'd get the visibility he'd need to keep the diner open."

"He said that?" I went to Ben's almost daily. Granted, it

wasn't packed, but there were always a handful of people in there when I'd go. He never mentioned that he needed money or was having problems.

"Yeah. I was the one who was the sucker and gave him charity. I even donated the damn milk from my dairy cows for the fresh food for the days that critic was coming." The chair squeaked when he leaned back, his coffee mug in his hands. "When I told Ben that we weren't going to use the high-dollar bamboo beams he wanted, he went off his rocker." Danny shook his head. "I had to remind him that I was doing this free of charge. That's when he decided to fire me from a charitable job."

He hesitated and stared at me for a second.

"From what I hear, his diner has been booming since they found that guy dead." He shrugged.

I decided to move on because I was going to have to check out this charity thing he was talking about.

"What about Finn's job?" I asked.

"That was a paying job, but I'm so busy here that I just couldn't hold up to my end of the deal. My guys are swamped. I dropped the ball. We don't usually do residential, so I put him on the back burner." His lips turned down. "I should've told him I couldn't do it, but I hated to turn him down. That good ole southern manners thing."

"I get it." I laughed.

"With a mama like Viv, I know you do." He winked. "I was glad to read in the paper that there's another suspect in the famous guy's death."

"Yeah." I blinked a few times. "No one has been charged yet."

"I know your mama didn't kill that critic. In fact, I'd just left her house with a special order of creamer she'd ordered. I was on my way over to The Tattered Cover Books and Inn to drop off some fresh milk to that chef Ben had hired."

"You were taking milk to Mundy?" I asked.

"Yep." His lips drew together. He got up and walked over to the filing cabinet. He pulled out a yellow piece of paper. "Your mama showed up here around four. I told her it would take a half hour or so to pull the freshest cream, so we made plans for me to drop it off at her house. I knew I needed to make a drop-off to Mundy and it was on my way."

He shut the file cabinet drawer back and walked over to me with the paper in his hand.

"This is an order form for fresh creamer. We have to log the heifer number, the time of day, and the creaming process. We can't pull too much milk out of our heifers at one time so we can produce the freshest milk, cream, butter," he shrugged, "anything that's made with the milk. Your mama insisted I get her the freshest we had and she'd pay top dollar."

He handed me the order slip.

"Can I get a photo of this?" I asked and pulled out my phone when he nodded. The thought lingered in my head that some people still thought Mama to be a suspect, so I wanted to make it very clear from the timeline that she didn't kill anyone.

"You can see from the timestamp I pulled the cream from the stock at four-thirty, so by the time I got to your mama's house it was around five. She was leaving when I got there. She paid me and I was on my way." He walked back around to his desk and sat down again.

"Do you have the order form from Chef Mundy?" I asked.

"Yeah. He's a strange one. Paid cash. Said he didn't want a receipt with his name or any identifying information." He shrugged and walked back over to the cabinet, pulling out another work order. "Of course, I made an order anyways. We have to for our records."

"Thanks, Danny." I took the paper from him and took a picture of it before I stood up. I pointed to the coffee pot for a refill and he nodded. "I appreciate the information."

"You need to tell that deputy of yours that Riley Titan doesn't have a work permit from the American Builders Association either," he muttered. My eyes narrowed. "Don't get me wrong. We need a residential contractor around here. We had our monthly ABA meeting and when I didn't see him I asked around. The president did a quick search in the ABA database and said he'd never heard of Riley Titan."

"Does he have to be a member in order to do the work?" I had to admit I wasn't very well informed on the laws of construction. Suddenly I remembered Mrs. Brown saying something about Danny trying to beat up Riley.

"He doesn't have to be a member, but it's hard to get a job without good credentials. Maybe not when you're in a hurry like Ben," he said.

"I'll make a note of it. Though I did hear you went to Finn's to sock Riley in his clock." I took a sip of the coffee.

"Are you kidding me?" He rolled his eyes and let out a disgusted humph. "That guy is crazy. I went there to pick up my tools that were left behind. I asked him about his job permit that he needed to file with the city. He shoved me first. Mrs. Brown was being nosy as usual and I just let it go. I'm not the construction police."

"I'll be sure to tell Finn to make sure there's a permit." I still had a question for him. "One more thing." I stopped before I walked out the door and turned around. "Do you know anything about a Botox scheme going down at the condo complex on the river?" I asked.

"What the hell is Botox?" Confusion crossed his face.

"It's something dermatologists or licensed professionals put in women's wrinkles to make them disappear. Mama went to one of the condos and got who-knows-what injected into her face because she wanted to look good on TV. She said she got it from someone living in your condo complex." I still had to follow up on it, even though I wanted to follow up on the Ben lead Danny had just given me.

"I don't know a thing about that kind of stuff, but you'd have to have the condo owner's permission. They own their condo; I just keep up the HOA responsibilities like keeping the landscape nice, the buildings in great working condition, and doing any repairs. " His eyes blazed and rolled over me. "Don't be going and making trouble. I don't feel like going behind you and making any angry residents there happy."

"Thanks for the coffee." I held the cup in the air and headed on out of the barn.

I started up the Jeep and sat there for a second collecting my thoughts. My stomach growled. I knew what I had to do and I hated it. I hated all of it. I needed to call Finn and let him know what Danny had told me. If he was right, the work Riley was doing might not be legal. I knew how much Finn wanted to get the work finished. With Riley not having the right paperwork, it could set back the addition even longer.

What on earth was he talking about Ben and charity? Jolee and Ben had both mentioned he needed the publicity and that business was down, but was he in dire straits? Though Mundy was now our number one suspect, I couldn't just ignore the strange behavior Ben had displayed, nor the fact that he was all too happy his business had picked up since Frank's death.

My heart sank. Ben and Mundy were friends. Had they staged the fight? The whole thing? Were they in on this together?

"Hey, Betty." I grabbed the walkie-talkie off my passenger seat since I didn't have on my uniform. I decided to go ahead and call in to dispatch to check out what Finn had found out with Mundy. "Is Finn there?" I was sure he'd already dragged Mundy in for questioning this morning.

"No, he ran over to Dixon's because Toots said there were three cars there this morning with those handicap tags," she said.

"Did he bring anyone in for questioning?" I asked.

"Not here he didn't," she said.

"All right. I'll try calling his cell." The only way to know for sure if Ben and Mundy were in cahoots was to pay Chef Mundy a visit. As sheriff, I had no time to play around with fake tags. I might've been removed from the case, but I had to know.

"Kenni." Betty's mom voice came through. "You aren't going to go see Mundy, are you?"

"Maybe," I muttered. "Finn told you about Mundy?"

"He came in here first thing and wrote down all the information on that darn whiteboard. I can read." She laughed. "If I read between the lines, it means that Viv isn't the number one suspect anymore."

"There's nothing wrong with your eyes," I joked. "I'm not sure I can wait until Mayor Ryland decides to give me back the lead. But I'm going to head on over to check out my leads on the Botox scheme. Let Finn know when he gets back."

"Will do, Sheriff." Betty clicked off the walkie-talkie.

Chapter Twenty-Four

"I told you that there's something about that chef." Poppa appeared in the passenger seat.

"Just like everything else we know, it's all just talking out loud and trying to fit pieces of a puzzle to make it whole," I reminded him.

"You've got to check out the pieces before you can put them in the puzzle." Poppa's voice held tension. It was his way of telling me to go see Mundy.

"Unfortunately, I have a job to do. I want Finn to succeed, so I'm going to let him take the lead with Mundy. In the meantime, I need to go check out the condos," I reminded him and turned on Poplar Holler Road.

"Then he should be checking out Mundy before he goes on some goofy goose chase about some handicap stickers." Poppa shrugged. "Who cares if people want to park closer? It's not life or death like keeping a killer on the street."

I slid my eyes to the country road ahead of me, biting the edge of my lip. It was time to get to the bottom of the Botox scheme and get them shut down. Then I'd take on Mundy. I was the sheriff in this town and it was about time Mayor Ryland knew it.

"One crime at a time. Botox first. Mundy next." I gave a sideway glance towards Poppa.

"Now we're talking." Poppa bounced in the seat.

I wasn't going to lie. There was a renewed fire in my soul

that I'd seemed to have lost over the past twenty-four hours. This was my town. I was in charge and I was going to solve this murder.

The old road ran along the Kentucky River. It was a great place to live if you wanted a relaxing view and to be away from everyone. The condominiums were a sore spot with many locals.

I was one of the people who were pro-condos. I figured it'd be filled with retired folks who'd want a pretty view and an easy rest of their lives in our little town. There'd never been any problems that I remembered and there still weren't. In fact, no one had complained.

I sure would hate to go in there guns a'blazing with no knowledge about the stuff. Nor was I sure that what they were doing was illegal. Today the view of the river was a little more skewed with the rain, but it was still pretty. The limestone walls along the river weren't like anything else. The trees along the riverbank were starting to get their leaves and the grass was starting to grow. The river was a little more churned up than normal, and once it settled the fishermen would be out in full force.

I pulled into one of the guest parking spots and grabbed my phone. Camille Shively would be the best person to ask my many questions.

"Twanda, it's Kenni. Is Camille there?" I asked Twanda Jakes, Camille's receptionist.

"Hi, Kenni. Hold on, I'll see if she's free. We've been slammed with this sudden onset of the flu." She put me on hold and replaced the silence with some rock instrumental that made my toe tap.

"Hey, Kenni. What's going on?" Camille answered.

"I'm not sure if you are aware, but there's been something called a Botox party going on in Cottonwood. I'm not real sure about the medical laws and before I shut it down, is it illegal for the everyday schmo to inject it?" I asked.

"Kenni," she gasped. "I've had so many patients coming in with muscle aches, a few with fever, soreness, runny nose, dizziness, and fatigue. I've been treating them for the flu, but if you say there's someone doing illegal Botox, they could have Botox poisoning

"Poisoning?" My heart sank down into my once tapping toe.

"Yes. Only a medically trained person or a physician who is board certified by the American Board of Plastic Surgery can administer Botox. They'll have a license to prove it too. Kenni..." The pause in her voice sent a shiver down my spine. "This is very serious. I'm going to have to call all the patients who I diagnosed with the flu."

"Can you send a list of those names to the department? I'm going to need them as witnesses after I arrest these people." I stared at the condo complex. "Are these people in danger of dying?"

"If they get enough of it in their system." I could feel the tension in her voice. "Listen, Kenni, I've got to go. Let me know if I can be of more help. I'll have Twanda get those names over to Betty."

She hung up the phone before I could even say goodbye. I looked at the complex and noticed the front of it was all the front doors of each condo. Since I'd never been there, I figured the view was all in the back since that was where the river was and the enticement to buy a condo there.

"This isn't exactly the kind of crime I wanted to help you on." I jumped when Poppa appeared.

"You just scared me to death." I held my heart. "Maybe that's your plan. Be here to take me to the great beyond."

"Don't be ridiculous. I'm obviously here to help you solve Frank Von Lee's murder and here you are doing this Botox thing." He rolled his eyes. "Hurry on in there and get them in jail so we can get to the real crime."

"This is a crime. People could die." I contemplated whether or not to call Finn in case I needed backup. I also wanted to hear his voice and get some information about why Mundy wasn't in the cell at the department.

"I'm going to go on in." He ghosted away.

I scrolled through my phone. The pad of my thumb hovered over the call button. A couple of times I went to push it but pulled back. I didn't need to check up on him. I had to give him the chance to get Mundy.

The sheer thought of seeing him sent electric energy through me. A long deep sigh escaped me. I grabbed my bag from the backseat and pulled my gun out of it along with my handcuffs. My badge was clipped on my visor and I pulled it off and clipped it on the neck of my sweatshirt. When I got out of the Jeep, I stuck my gun in the waistband of my jeans, my phone in one of my back pockets, and my cuffs in the other.

There wasn't any immediate danger so I didn't call Finn. Instead, I set an alarm to signal me not to forget about my cake class. There was no way I was missing out on how to make cute flowers.

The building appeared to have ten condos on each level. If I was right, twenty-two would be on the third floor. Instead of taking the elevator, I decided to take the stairs. Adrenaline was coursing through my veins and jogging up steps would help get that under control.

The stairs were locked off with a keypad next to them. I ran my finger down the names of the residents to see if I recognized any of them. I had nothing.

"That place is crazy in there." Poppa appeared, making me jump again.

"Can't you like ring a bell or something before you show up? I never know when you're going to appear." My words were probably a little harsh, but it was true. He was going to take me back with him if I wasn't careful.

"Ding, ding." Poppa acted like he was tapping a bell. "Is that better?"

"Thank you." I laughed. "I'm trying to figure out who's going to ring me in."

"If you are Kim from Clay's Ferry, you can press number twenty-two." He did his little jig.

"Kim from Clay's Ferry." I grinned. "You saw the client list."

"I did. Your mama's name is on the list on the day of Frank Von Lee's murder like she said. There are two recliners. Two women are injecting the stuff in these women's faces. It's really gross." Poppa made a blech face. "Whaddya say we go and arrest these women so we can get on with the real investigation?"

I dragged my finger down the list of numbers on the intercom and pushed twenty-two.

"Yes," the woman answered through the intercom.

"Kim from Clay's Ferry," I said and turned to Poppa, who was no longer there.

"Come up." The sound of a buzz followed.

I grabbed the door handle and jerked it open. On the way up the two flights, I took two steps at a time. It was the second condo down the hall. I put my ear to the door before I knocked to try and hear if anything was going on. According to Poppa, there were two women in there getting poked and prodded.

"Ding, ding!" Poppa was taking it a little too far now.

I still jumped. "Seriously?"

"I ding, I don't ding. Which is it?" he asked.

"What's going on in there?" I asked in a hushed whisper. I took the clipped badge off my shirt and stuck it on the waistband of my jeans next to my gun. They probably wouldn't be so willing to let me in with a badge.

"From what I gather, the scheme is two women. In the

back-right room, there is a lamination machine, a printer, and a computer. They're making the handicap tags in there. They told one of the women that's getting her lips all plumped up that since she's had surgery she can upgrade to the handicap package for another hundred dollars," he said.

"Hundred dollars?" I asked in shock.

"Kim from Clay's Ferry?" The woman jerked the door open and there I was with my mouth hanging open. She jerked her head out the door and looked both ways. "Who were you talking to?"

"Myself." I faked a smile. "I was talking myself into this."

"You need your elevens done bad," she snarled. "I thought you said you wanted your crow's feet, but I think you need a good dose in between them eyes." Her eyes darted around my face. "Or we can do both. It's gonna cost you."

"Can I come in?" I asked.

She dragged the door open and I stepped inside. It was exactly how Poppa had described it. The entire condo was empty except for two chairs and a table. On the table there were some glass bottles, needles, and some rubbing alcohol. There was nothing legal about this. The two women in the chairs were leaned back.

"You're a little early, so you can just stand over there and enjoy the view." She pointed to the windows.

There was an amazing view of both sides of the river. It was still spitting rain and cloudy.

"I'm sorry." I turned around. The woman was bent over the client and using a magnifying glass attached to the chair to get a close-up view of the wrinkles. "Do you have a restroom?"

"Down the hall." She didn't look up. Neither of them did.

I walked down the hall and looked over my shoulder to see if they were watching me. They weren't. The room that Poppa said was the room where they made the handicap hangers was behind a closed door. I walked down the hall to where the bathroom was and slipped my hand around to the door handle. I pushed in the lock and pulled it closed just in case they came looking for me.

I tiptoed back to the shut door where the printing was happening and slowly turned the handle so they wouldn't hear me. After I pushed it open, I put my hand on the other side of the door and slowly turned the knob. It was never a good thing to be caught snooping around. The door gave a slight swoosh when I closed it.

My hand dragged up the wall to find the light switch, exposing the shenanigans. It was exactly what Poppa had said. I took my phone out of my pocket and snapped several photos of all the evidence I was going to need to lock these crazy people up. It already set up to print when I shook the mouse on the mousepad to wake up the sleeping computer. There were already a few tags printed and ready to go. There was a cashbox next to the printer. I opened it and it was filled with twenties and fives. I could hear Myrna now saying how it was twenty-five dollars. This was an all-cash scheme from what I could see. Perfect for not being able to trace it back to them and easy to keep the scheme going from city to city.

After I'd taken enough photos, I scrolled through my contacts to find Danny's number. With my hand over the microphone, when he answered, I said, "Hey, Danny. It's Kenni again. I'm sorry to bug you, but can you tell me who owns number twenty-two in your condo complex?"

"You know what, Kenni, I don't know any of the people who bought condos, but I can tell you that number twenty-two was never purchased, along with number eight. Why? Are you in the market? I can probably give our good sheriff a deal." He was always doing business.

"No one owns it?" I asked.

"No wonder they are going unnoticed." Poppa appeared. "Oh, ding." He laughed.

I glared.

"Thanks, Danny. I'm sorry about earlier. I'm just narrowing things down." I hung up the phone and looked at Poppa. "They are illegally squatting here and doing Botox, plus these." I pointed to the tags.

"Now you go get them." Poppa marched to the door.

"You're right, but first I need to call Betty so she'll be on the ready in case I need some backup." I scrolled down to the dispatch and pushed the call button. I quickly explained to Betty what I was doing and that I'd probably be bringing in two women to stick in the jail, so I'd need her to make a call to the sheriff in Clay's Ferry to let them know to expect a couple of transfers. They had a bigger jail that was equipped for more than one occupant.

I didn't bother trying to be quiet on my way back down the hall. I pulled my badge off my waistband and clipped it back on the neck of my sweatshirt.

"All right. Stop what you're doing." I pulled up my sweatshirt to expose my gun. "You two are under arrest for illegally living here. That's called squatting. Not to mention the illegal making of handicap tags and selling illegal Botox."

"Illegal Botox?" Polly Parker, of all people, flung up from one of the chairs. Her mother was in the other.

Polly's blonde hair was tugged up in a top knot on top of her head. Her face was pale and splotchy, not the normal flawless-looking skin I was used to. Goes to show you what a little makeup could do.

"Step aside, you two." I gestured to the women. "Polly, Mrs. Parker, you stay where you are."

The women were very cooperative. Neither of them said a word to me or each other as I cuffed them wrist to wrist and read them their rights. If I had two sets of cuffs, I'd have cuffed them separately.

"Kenni," Mrs. Parker's southern drawl was a lot deeper than normal, "we wouldn't want it to get out that we were here doing anything illegal. If you know what I mean."

Yeah. I knew what she meant. She knew it was illegal and she didn't want anyone to know that she was an active participant and wanted me to keep my mouth shut.

"Uh-huh," Polly grunted. I wasn't sure, but I don't think she could speak. Her lips were so big and red that her mouth finally matched her horse teeth. Unfortunately, her lips took up her petite face.

"We were getting a little touch up for the engagement photos." Mrs. Parker tried to squint her eyes a couple of times, but when nothing moved she gave up offering a sweet southern bless-your-heart smile that I knew all too well.

"You were here under illegal pretenses, and I just can't think you thought this was all right." I motioned at the needles. "Dr. Shively has several patients that have come down with flu symptoms. When a bad batch of Botox is administered, these symptoms pop up. Not to mention their illegal shenanigans with the pink handicap tags."

"Honey," Mrs. Parker walked over to the women, "how long until I can move my eyes?"

"Mrs. Parker, please make an appointment to go see Dr. Shively and she can give you and Polly all the details." I wouldn't let her speak to the women. "If you and Polly don't mind coming down to the station to give a statement, I'd be mighty grateful."

"Oh, we can't do that, right, Mama?" Polly muttered under her puffy, fluffy lips.

"Right. I told you that we don't want to be associated." Mrs. Parker tugged on Polly. "Let's go."

"I'm sorry, I'm going to have to insist that you come to the department to give a statement." I tried to be nice the first time. They just weren't getting it.

"And what if we don't?" Mrs. Parker pulled her shoulders back. Her eyelids tried to move up and down, but she gave up.

"Then y'all will be sitting in the back of Cowboy's Catfish with these two." The timer on my phone chirped that I had one hour until I had to leave for my cake class. "What's it going to be?"

"If I give a very generous donation to your next campaign, is there any way you can at least not use our names?" she asked.

"I'll not use your names when Edna Easterly comes calling," I agreed.

"Wonderful. We will come down later after we put some frozen peas on our faces and see Dr. Shively." Mrs. Parker tilted her head to the door, signaling for Polly to follow.

"All right, you two, let's go," I instructed them as I dialed in dispatch. "Betty, it's Kenni. I'm bringing in the two women. Call Danny Shane and let him know that he can't touch or even show condo number twenty-two. It's officially a crime scene. Call the Clay's Ferry sheriff and let him know that we've got two transports."

The women cursed and fussed all the way to the Jeep. I uncuffed them, draped the cuffs around the door handle, and cuffed them again. This way I could go grab the evidence that was there. I grabbed my bag that had all the evidence bags and headed back inside. Going up and down the stairs to and from the Jeep was great exercise. I carried the copy machine, all the Botox stuff, and all the handicap tags and put them in the back of the Jeep. After I felt like I'd taken enough photos and all the evidence there was, I decided it was time to take them to jail.

I stuck them in the back and didn't bother turning on the siren. The less attention drawn on me, the better. This way I still had just enough time to get to my class. Later I'd go back to the department after they were transported and write my report, not to mention update Mama's timeline that Poppa wanted me to do so badly.

"I bet your mama ratted on us." One of the women cursed at me from the backseat.

"Actually she didn't." I looked in the rearview mirror at her. "This whole thing would've been over by now if she had."

"So they remember her?" Poppa appeared next to me in the front seat. He was turned around facing the women. "Ask them."

"You do remember my mama then?" I asked.

"What's in it for us if we talk to you?" the other one asked in a curious tone.

"If you cooperate, then I have the authority to ask the judge to go easy on you." It was true.

I played it nonchalant, careful not to lay out all my cards.

"Yeah. I remember her." The first one chimed in but not without getting a hard elbow to her ribs from the other woman. "What? I don't want to go to jail forever."

The Jeep sped down Poplar Holler Road and when I got to the stop sign that led me back into town, I put the gear in park and turned around in my seat.

"Tell me what you know." I looked directly at the one who was ready to talk.

"She came in two days in a row. It's hard to forget someone when they come like that." She smiled. "It wasn't really that that caught my attention because Melanie here was her injector." She nodded toward the other woman. "Anyways, she was upset and she mentioned between her tears that her daughter was the sheriff. Anything doing with the law freaks us out." She gave me a hard look. "That's when I spoke up and told her I'd refund her handicap fee that she paid for the first time she was here if she didn't say anything about her visit to our little party."

"She didn't either. What time was it when she came in the

second day?" I can't believe Mama wanted a handicap tag so badly.

"She came around suppertime." She held her free hand in the air and gave the so-so gesture by waving it side to side. "Six-ish."

"My mama was in a bit of a pickle. She's been placed at a homicide scene. Though she's not the number one suspect anymore, it's good to know her whereabouts in case her timeline is questioned." I turned back around and put the gearshift into drive. "Are you willing to go on record with this information?"

"Only if you can help us," Melanie chimed in.

"I'm good for my word." There was a bit of relief that now I had a true timeline and two witnesses for Mama. I only wanted to make sure all my T's were crossed and I's were dotted when it came to Frank and Mama.

"This is good." Poppa rubbed his hands together and bounced a little in his seat. "I'm glad you didn't listen to this old coot." His eyes dipped. "I know I'm here to guide you. I'm sorry for overstepping my boundaries."

Oh, how I wished I could hug a ghost.

Chapter Twenty-Five

The Clay's Ferry sheriff's deputy was already at the office by the time I got the two women down there. The deputy waited while I fingerprinted them and took down all their information. I let them know about the process and how they'd be taken to court in the morning for their full charges. They'd have to wait to make their one phone call until they got to Clay's Ferry. I assured them I'd let the judge know about their cooperation, and I was a woman of my word. Even though I had the ledger with Mama's name, I still wanted a written statement. They wrote them while I finished up the transfer paperwork and gave it to the Clay's Ferry deputy.

"Ya know," Melanie said to me before the deputy took them away, "you really should think about getting those elevens filled in." She pointed to the creases between my eyes.

I motioned for the deputy to take them. Betty sat there taking it all in. It was prime gossip for her and she got a front-row seat to all of it.

"Elevens?" Betty asked.

"Don't ask." I rolled my eyes but couldn't help dragging the pad of my finger down the creases. "Give Edna Easterly a call and let her know about this case. It's a scoop she can put in the Chronicle. Tell her that I'll send her the police report tonight." I grabbed the laptop off of my desk. If there was some downtime at the cake class like I'd had at the last class, I'd quickly jot down some of the notes about the case.

On the forty-five minute drive to Lexington, I figured I'd better get in touch with Finn.

"Hey there," he answered.

"You aren't going to believe what just went down." It was strange that he was working one investigation while I was doing another. I knew that his disappointment in my lack of judgement, though it was just temporary, hurt me personally.

This was always my fear in dating him. I had to keep the work stuff separate from the personal stuff. His feelings were just work stuff and I needed to get a little thicker skin in this department of my life. I would apologize to Finn and make it right when I saw him. But for now, I needed to catch him up on the fake handicap investigation.

"Tell me."

"I busted the fake handicap sticker ring. It was two women operating from the condos out on Poplar Holler. They were squatting in a condo there doing illegal tags and Botox." I never would've believed this type of thing would ever go on in Cottonwood.

"Botox?" he asked.

"Yep. That's what Mama had done to her face. Remember when we saw her at Ben's the morning of Frank's death?" I asked.

"Oh man. You did point it out that she looked different," he said.

"That's not all." I took a deep breath. "That's how she got the black eye. She was having a reaction."

"That's so weird the handicap scheme was tied in with that. Toots will be happy that all her handicap parking spaces in front of Dixon's will be open," he joked. "I'm glad they finished out your mama's timeline, but you know that she's not our number-one suspect anymore so you can stop proving it."

"Then we probably should meet up and talk about it."

"How about we get together tonight for dinner at the department and go over things?" His word were music to my ears.

"That sounds so good. Let's meet at the department around seven because I've got to finish a report about those illegal handicap tags."

"Are you sure?" he asked.

"I'm positive. I want you to fill me in on how Frank's case is going," I said.

"Mundy wasn't home when I went over there. I figured I'd hit it again before the end of the day," he said.

We exchanged a few more back and forth comments before we hung up.

The drive to Lexington wasn't so bad after that. I was looking forward to learning how to make flowers for my cake and seeing Finn. It was nice to get a parking spot right in front of Le Fork.

The instructor was putting everyone's covered cakes in front of them. I'd had no idea that it helped to decorate them cold from the fridge. It was so interesting and I'm sure that's why I enjoyed the class. I loved to learn and it also seemed to help me relax, which was something I really needed.

After I peeled off the cling wrap, I noticed my poor cakes had a peak at the top and everyone else had perfectly flat and even cakes. I draped the wrap back over so I didn't have to look at it.

"Today we are going to learn to properly ice a cake by making your very own buttercream icing. We are going to do a stiffening recipe and then we are going to thin it down so it spreads a little easier." The instructor smiled at everyone.

There were ingredients in little bowls at my station. She went through what was in each little bowl. There was shortening, butter flavoring, water, milk, cane sugar, meringue powder (whatever that was), and salt. She instructed us to add the ingredients using a hand mixer, which proved to be a little difficult for me.

"Ding, ding!" Poppa smacked his leg and cackled. "You can handle a gun perfectly but not a mixer?" He bent over in laughter. "You don't take after your mama."

Then a light bulb went off in my head. Was I trying so hard to be accepted by Mama? Or having something that both of us could do together? Everyone knew she wasn't happy with my career choice, and as the years ticked by she wasn't getting any better about it. Just crazier.

I ignored Poppa and firmly grabbed the mixture, determined to get this right. The instructor had already moved on to what she referred to as a cake leveler. Apparently, it was supposed to even out the top of my lopsided cake. I basically used the tool to saw the peak of my cakes off, making them level. I had no idea so much went into baking a cake. I had a newfound respect for bakers.

The instructor was going so fast. When I looked around, it was only me that was going slow. Everyone else had already gotten an icing bag and attached a tip with a coupler. The only one left for me to pick was the one with the big round hole. We had to make a ring of icing around the top of the cake and fill in the middle with fruit of our choice. Since it was my first cake, I decided to give it to Mama and added strawberries in the middle because they was her favorite.

I put one cake on top of the other and did the same thing, making it a two-layer strawberry cake. Next was the icing part. She asked us to be very generous with the buttercream with her technique of covering the entire cake using the flat end of the spatula to smooth it out. She gave us a short potty break to let our icing set. Some people chose to put a second coat of icing on, but I didn't. She showed us how to use the edge of a knife to go around the sides of the cake to make the ridge pattern. We used another bag of tinted icing to make an icing ring around the cake.

"That's all for today." The instructor untied her apron and put it aside.

"I thought we were learning to do flowers?" I asked.

"That's a little too in depth for a group class, but if you'd like a private lesson, I'm more than happy to do that." She nodded. "You know how to bake and ice your cake now so you can do those at home and come back with them for a lesson in flower making."

"I can do that." It was decided. I'd give Mama this cake and to surprise Finn, I'd give him the one with the flowers. "Yes. I'll do that."

"I'm free in a couple of days," she noted, looking at her calendar that was lying on her workstation. "About the same time?"

"Sure." This made me happy. I knew Mama was not the killer and Finn was no longer disappointed in me.

Life would be perfect after I found Mundy and arrested him for the murder of Frank Von Lee.

Chapter Twenty-Six

A couple of hours later, I'd dropped off my cake to my parents. They weren't home so I left it there with a note. They were probably out taking a drive or heading out of town for supper. Mama was still laying low and I couldn't wait to get her off the hook.

Duke had been home all day, though Mrs. Brown was letting him out. I decided to pick him up and take him to the department with me. We parked in front of Cowboy's Catfish. The home-cooked fried food smelled good and I was starving.

Bartleby Fry was slinging burgers in the back while talking to the customers through the pass-through. Duke headed straight to the kitchen because he knew Bartleby was always good for a treat. Not just any treat, a real piece of meat, which I rarely gave him at home.

"To what do I owe the pleasure of a front door visit?" Bartleby asked after I'd pushed through the swinging kitchen door.

"I want two fried catfish platters to go," I said, looking at the plated food on the pass-through window, trying not to let the drool run out of my mouth. "Extra tartar sauce and fries, please."

"You got it." He flipped a piece of something to Duke. "I'll bring it over. Coffee or Diet Coke?"

"Both." I winked and headed to the door that was between the restaurant and the department. Duke wasn't going to budge and I knew Bartleby would bring him over with my food.

Betty had left for the day. I flipped on the lights and immediately started to fill out the paperwork on the Botox arrest. My photos from my phone had already synched to the Google photo application we'd started using at the department. Finn had suggested all sorts of new technology that was truly helpful. I attached the photos to the report along with a scanned copy of their statement about Mama. Before I hit send, I read the report carefully.

The clock on the wall told me it was almost time for Finn to meet me here.

"Yep. He'll be here in a minute, so get up and start that timeline." Poppa stood next to the dry-erase board.

"I do want to get some things laid out before he gets here." I looked back at the door of Cowboy's when I could smell the fish frying. It wouldn't be long until he brought the food over.

I hit send on the document to the judge along with the report on the Botox case. I got up and grabbed the black dry-erase marker. I dragged the wet tip of the marker horizontally across the board. I completely filled in Mama's timeline where there were holes. Her whereabouts were all accounted for.

"Okay." Poppa paced back and forth. "Now make a line for Mundy." He pointed. "We know he was at Ben's in the morning when you went with Finn."

I began to fill out Mundy's timeline and put bullet points of his history and why he was our number one suspect.

"Malina saw Mundy at the hotel." I tapped the felt of the marker on the board.

"Don't forget about Danny Shane delivering milk to Mundy at the hotel around five," Poppa reminded me.

"I almost forgot about that!" I snapped my fingers and wrote that down. "What was he doing between five thirty and seven?"

"Forgot about what?" Finn stood at the door of the department with Duke. "Who are you talking to?" he questioned.

"Myself." I reddened. Poppa disappeared. I snapped the lid back on the marker and walked over to Finn. "Duke." My trusty bloodhound ran over, shoving his nose in my pocket where he thought I had a treat.

"Here boy." Finn grabbed a treat off the desk and flipped it towards Duke.

At first I was a little timid about how to approach Finn since there'd been so much tension between us about even the thought of hiding evidence. I put all of that aside and walked over to him. He stared at me the entire time and our eyes never looked away.

"I stopped by the house to see how Riley was doing." He smiled.

"And?" I teased.

"He was doing great." He reached out for my hands. "The new addition is coming along."

"Be sure that his permit is displayed in the window because the Beautification Committee love to drive around and nab people." I'd completely forgotten to tell him about that.

"What do they do?" He laughed.

"It's the law to have a permit, but they get to keep some of the fine the judge will give the contractor. Their part of the fine goes into the committee and they use it to do projects, so they're always on the lookout. They get money anyway they can," I told him.

Those members were ruthless. Once they dinged me for the new fence I'd put up for Duke.

"I missed you today," I whispered and curled up on my tippy toes.

We hugged each other and melted into a warm kiss. The

fluttering started in my throat and didn't stop until it reached my toenails.

"I'm sorry I ever had you doubt my moral compass. I'd never ever hold evidence in a case. Even involving my mama." Even though we'd already gotten past it last night, I felt like I needed to say it one last time.

"You shouldn't be sorry. I knew you'd never do anything to jeopardize your career or your mother. It was a knee-jerk reaction on my part." He didn't let me protest. He simply pulled me tighter and kissed me harder.

"Ahem." Bartleby cleared his throat. "Don't mind me. I'm just delivering the best damn fried fish in the state."

I waved my hand in the air but didn't dare pull away from Finn. Bartleby walking in on us wasn't that big of a deal, but a ninety-pound bloodhound was hard to ignore when he pushed his way in between us.

"Are you feeling left out, buddy?" Finn laughed and looked down.

Duke gave a low playful groan followed up by a big yawn. Happy he'd come between us, he sauntered over to his big pillow bed and laid down.

"I'm starving." I rubbed my hands together. "And that food smells so good."

Bartleby had put the two Styrofoam containers on my desk along with two cups of coffee and two fountain drink Diet Cokes.

"Me too." Finn's hand drew down my back. He guided me over to the food.

It was dead silent when we opened the containers and eyed the delicious-looking food. We each took one and dug in.

"I see you've been working on a timeline." Finn smiled. "You thought it was a stupid idea at first."

"I never thought it was stupid. I thought it was a waste of time. But as you can see, I filled in Mama's." My brows rose. "I started Mundy's and was getting ready to start one for Ben."

"I thought you were staying off the case," he reminded me.

"I had to clear Mama. But I can still lend a hand and my two cents. I feel like I need to get in touch with Mundy in order to clear Ben's name." I gnawed on the end of the straw from the Diet Coke and waited for Finn's response.

"Yeah." He took a drink of his Coke. "That thought about Ben crossed my mind only because his business has been so good since all of this. Plus I went down to the bank and found out that they were about to call in his loan because he's not been able to pay full rent." Finn walked over to the white board. He popped the hush puppy in his mouth before he picked up a dry erase marker and wrote Ben's name under the suspect list.

When he swiped a line across Mama's name, it took everything in me not to jump for joy. Instead, I stuffed my face with a big piece of fish dipped in the homemade tater sauce. I chewed with happiness.

"I hate to think that Ben could do something like that, but you have to think about it." Finn started his spiel, "Ben had hired Danny Shane for the construction. When I went to see Danny, he said that Ben fired him after he told Ben that the price was more than he'd thought and Ben was going to have to come up with the extra money before he could finish the job."

Danny had left that part out when I'd gone to see him and he told me was doing the work for free.

"I'm thinking Ben got in the oh-no-what-am-I-going-to-do mode. He got a little crazy and his fuse was short, so when Mundy refused to cook the way Ben wanted him to, he fired him." Finn seemed a little stuck.

I helped him get more stuck.

"Why would Ben kill Frank? That's where I'm stumped." I eyed the board.

"Or we can find Mundy and see what he has to say." Finn

cocked a brow. "I went by there again. I wonder if he's on the lam."

"Mundy would have more of a motive than Ben. It would make sense if he thought we were getting hot on his trail, or if he saw the headlines in the Chronicle where Mayor Ryland said we had more than one suspect." I took the marker from Finn and I wrote as I talked. "According to Guy from the Frank's class, Mundy's career almost never happened because he and Frank got into a fight. Mundy got arrested. There's an arrest record. Just by chance Mundy happened to call Ben for a job right in time for Frank's visit to the diner?"

"Very interesting." Finn stepped back and took a long look at the board. "I'll go to Le Fork in the morning and question them."

"Sure, but I've been there and talked to the people who worked there. Same thing. Mundy was a jerk and no one liked him." I walked over to my computer and pulled up a new note to put in Frank's case about the information Jolee had snuck out of Mundy's file, leaving the part out about how I'd gotten the info.

Chapter Twenty-Seven

Even with Finn and me spending more time together, I didn't sleep any better. Ben was on my mind and I was sad that he could possibly have killed Frank.

With thoughts of him and trying to figure out a true motive other than money, I tossed and turned all night with images of kissing Finn. We didn't end up leaving the office until well past midnight. It was so cute how he followed me home, even though he had to go that way to go home too. He took it a step further and parked in front of my house, waiting for me to make it inside. Such a southern boyfriend thing to do. He was really fitting in well here.

I flipped over and looked at the clock, turning off my alarm before it even went off. Duke lifted his head as though he was anticipating my next move. He'd even gotten tired of my antsy bed rolling and laid on the floor most of the night. He jumped up when I peeled back the covers.

"Let's go outside." I patted his head and we headed down the hall.

When I let him out, the warmer temperature swooshed in the door even though it was still dark out. I locked the door behind him, flicked on the coffee maker, and padded down the hall to grab my shower.

He'd be out there sniffing around, giving me enough time to get ready.

Five minutes later, I'd showered and thrown on my sheriff's

uniform. Today I opted for a short-sleeved button-up shirt instead of the tee. It was a hair-pulled-up-in-a-ponytail morning. With a swipe of lip gloss and my walkie-talkie strapped on my shoulder, I was ready.

"Betty," I called across the walkie-talkie when I made my way back down the hall into the kitchen.

"Hey, Sheriff. What ya been doing this morning?" Betty asked in an upbeat voice.

The aroma from the coffee smelled so good. I poured a cup and leaned against the counter, staring out into my kitchen. Poppa wasn't here.

"I'm just getting ready to make my rounds." My thoughts turned to Finn. "Do you know where Finn is? I need to talk to him about the Frank Von Lee case." I let go of the button. The entire thing about me knowing where Mundy lived and me not telling him how was weighing on me. That was just another thing I shouldn't keep from him.

"He's not been here yet either. It looks like he's been doing some doodlin' on that white board though." Betty clicked. "And it looks like your mama is off the hook."

"Actually..." I felt flushed. "We started working together again."

Duke scratched the door. I pushed off of the countertop and walked over to let him in. I noticed Mrs. Brown's back floodlight from her porch was already on. Duke walked in, licking his lips.

"Did Mrs. Brown throw you a treat?" I asked the ornery dog.

"Huh?" Betty asked.

"Nothing." My eyes drew up to the clock. "You haven't seen Finn?" I asked again just for good measure because he said that he was going to go to the office first thing and officially call the Mayor to put me back on as lead.

He had to do that to get me officially back on the case.

Really it only involved a detailed list of why Mama was no longer a suspect. We agreed that both of us together solving the murder was better than one especially now that we had the Botox and handicap sticker case solved.

"Now that I'm looking around, he might've been here." I could hear her shuffling some papers in the background. "There are a bunch of papers on his desk from the lab."

"Papers?" I asked. "What kind of papers?"

"Oh." Betty's voice escalated. "It's from the lab. And Mundy's name is on it."

"Betty." I grabbed my keys and holster. "I'll be right there."

Duke rushed to the door. He knew the drill. When I grabbed my holster, we were leaving.

"Not this morning, buddy." I bent down and rubbed his head before I gave him a scoop of his kibble, plus a little extra. "Mrs. Brown will let you out."

His ears drew back and his eyes drooped even more than usual. He sat down on his hind legs, pouting.

"You be good. If things go well, this case will be over soon." I tried not to look at him. Whenever he looked like that, it made me feel bad.

The sun was just popping up over the rooves on Free Row. The gate was still a little damp from the dew. Birds were already chirping and playing around. It was a warm welcome that spring was here and the morning chill would soon be replaced by warmer temperatures.

"Mrs. Brown?" I called when I opened the Wagoneer door. She was watching from somewhere over there.

"Morning, Kenni," her voice trilled. "I'm feeding the birds."

"That's so nice of you." I tried to hide my smile. She was so nosy. "I don't see you."

She popped up out of the bush from the corner of her house closest to mine.

"Here I am." Curlers tight around her head, her fist gripped the top of her housecoat.

"You're up awfully early." I glanced over the roof of the Jeep toward Finn's house. His Dodge Charger wasn't there, but it looked like Riley was already there working.

"I was just keeping an eye on the neighborhood." She fiddled with her fingers. "You know, now that you and Finn are living here, there's not much going on. You've cleaned up Free Row."

"Thanks, Mrs. Brown. Do you mind..." I started to say.

"I don't mind having Duke at all. He's good company to me." She finished my sentence. I wasn't sure if that was good or bad. Did I really have her watch him so much that she expected it?

It was still early enough that there was no traffic and all the stoplights were green. It took me a total of five minutes to get to downtown. I passed Cowboy's Catfish and drove up the street to Ben's. Briefly I stopped in front of his diner. There was a faint light coming from the back.

I jerked the Jeep into a spot on the opposite side of street and parked. There was no hesitation. I got out of the Wagoneer and ran across the street. Ben peeked his head out of the kitchen when he heard me knocking. A big smile on his face. Not that of a killer, I thought and smiled back.

"To what do I owe this pleasure?" he asked after he unlocked the door and let me in.

"Coffee." It was all he needed to hear before he waved me back. "I'd love a cup, but this is more of an official stop." Finn should've been here, but I was good at thinking on my toes. I needed to feel Ben out before I got my day started.

"Sure. What can I answer for you?" he asked, not a thought in his head that this official visit had to do with him.

He pointed me to the coffee maker on the kitchen counter

as he grabbed a couple of oven mitts and took out some golden brown biscuits.

"Why didn't you tell me about your financial issues?" I busied myself with pouring the coffee and adding a little creamer.

"Here you go." He put a biscuit on the counter next to me. "I'll take a cup."

I handed him mine and looked at him. He gave a flat smile. He lifted the cup to his mouth and took a sip. I got another cup and took the plate with the biscuit and walked over to the preparation island and sat down on the stool.

"You're not my business partner." He leaned back more and crossed his ankles. "It's not something I'm proud of. The rent is going up and I want to purchase the building from the Shane Company, but Danny Shane won't sell."

"Danny Shane owns the building?" Even though I was sheriff, I had no idea who owned what around here. "I assumed you owned it."

"No. So when I told him I needed the repairs done for the show, he was all too willing to do the stuff for free until he got into it and saw that it needed a whole lot more. That's when he told me I had to pay for the work. There's no way I could afford his price and that's when I hired Riley. He's half the price." He shook his head. "When I confronted Danny about it, he let it slip that he wanted me out to put another shop in town."

"I went to visit Danny Shane and he did say that he was doing the work for free, but he failed to mention he is the landlord or that he wanted you out." That raised suspicion, though not for the murder. He had an alibi. "By the looks of all the lines and the Chronicle, your business has picked up."

"Wait," he stopped me. "Do you think I had anything to do with Frank Von Lee's murder?" His brows furrowed.

"I just have to cross all the T's and dot the I's." I could see by the look on his face that he was hurt and mad. "When I heard you were in a financial bind, it only fit since Frank's reviews could either make or break a place. Bad press like Frank dying can be good press, and your business has picked up."

"Not enough to buy the building, Kenni." He huffed through his nose. "I honestly can't believe that you'd even think I could do something like that. Besides, if anyone has a perfect reason, it's Mundy."

"You mean the fact that Frank was his teacher?" I asked.

"You know about that?" he asked.

"I looked into Mundy and his background. He has the perfect motive. I'm going to head on over to his place this morning and question him." I looked down at the pat of butter that'd melted into a puddle on top of my biscuit.

"You better get a jump on it. He's an early riser and doesn't get home until late." Ben grabbed a Styrofoam cup from the counter and poured a cup of coffee.

"I'm sorry, Ben. It's just that I have to do my job and..." I stood up and picked up the biscuit.

"No need to apologize. I understand. I've got to figure out a way to keep this diner open. I can't rely on famous people dying to keep that door open." He held the cup out in front of him. "Even though Mundy is a jerk and hotheaded, I don't see him as a killer."

"People kill people out of the heat of passion. Almost lose their minds." I took the coffee and offered a grateful smile. I was so glad Ben wasn't sore at me. A lifelong friendship wasn't one to let go of and I was fortunate to have a great friend in him.

"The Culinary Channel is going to do a life story on Frank and they are going to come and do an interview."

"That's great. Maybe that'll bring in business," I said before I exited the kitchen.

"Kenni," he called for me through the pass-through

window. "I thought you were off the case. You aren't doing something you shouldn't, are you?"

"Nope." I shook my head. "Mama has a solid alibi and now that she's no longer a suspect, there's no reason I can't continue."

"Good deal." He smiled and nodded before I left.

There was no time to go to the office if Mundy was an early riser. I had to take the opportunity while I felt like I had it. According to the file, Mundy lived on the south side of Lexington, not too far from Le Fork and the shopping strip.

The sunny morning had turned back to grey. It was typical Kentucky spring weather. You never knew what mood Mother Nature was going to be in. A few drops of rain splattered on the windshield. I turned on the wipers.

The entire forty-five-minute drive I rehearsed the typical questions I was going to ask him. I'd even checked the batteries in my tape recorder so I could get the full interview on it. My plan was to be all friendly and tell him I needed him to answer some questions. Maybe throw in the cake-baking class I've been taking from Le Fork and establish a little trust between us.

The apartment complex wasn't the nicest I'd seen in Lexington. The buildings were brown and dull. Mundy lived in building five, apartment nine. There were a couple of unread papers on the doorstep. I gave a hard couple of knocks and backed up. There wasn't anyone around and he didn't answer.

Had he skipped town? I knocked again. The papers certainly appeared to show he'd not been here a couple of days. I knocked again, this time harder and a few more raps.

This time the door cracked open. I took the flashlight from my holster and used the butt to push the door open.

"Mundy?" I called into the apartment. "Mundy?" I asked again, a little louder as I stepped inside.

There wasn't any sort of movement or sound coming from

within. I put the flashlight back in the holster and exchanged it for my gun. I held my gun out in front of me just in case he was in there and going to pounce on me.

"Sheriff's department!" I yelled and moved swiftly through the rooms, securing them one by one. There was a kitchen that overlooked a small family room and a bathroom. "Mundy!"

It wasn't like I had jurisdiction over the Fayette county area and he didn't have to give up, but still, words had power. I turned my back toward the family room with my gun pointed down the hall. There were two doors, one on each side.

"Come out, Mundy! I'm here to talk to you about Frank Von Lee's murder!" I swung open the first door down the hallway on the right with the toe of my cowboy boot. My eyes darted around the bedroom before they focused on a pair of feet sticking out from the far side of the bed.

I stuck my gun in my holster on my way over to the body.

"Mundy," I gasped. There was a gun in his limp hand and a bullet wound in his head, or what was left of it. By the looks of it, he'd sat next to his bed and shot himself. There was brain matter splattered everywhere on the ground.

"Yeah. I guess we have our killer." Poppa ghosted next to me.

Chapter Twenty-Eight

"Why on earth did you come up here without telling me?" Finn asked, pulling me aside to let the Fayette County sheriff's department do their job.

"I was coming to the office because Betty told me that the evidence from the lab had come in, but I was waylaid by seeing Ben at his diner. I took the opportunity to go in there and question him. He obviously didn't kill Frank. He confirmed that he knew Mundy and Mundy did have the motive. He also told me that Mundy was an early riser so I took the opportunity." My stomach dropped as the coroner took Mundy's body out of the apartment.

I bowed my head and said a silent prayer for him as he went to the great beyond as they passed me.

"I really wished you'd called me." Finn studied me thoughtfully.

"Well, I sorta went ahead and took the lead back," I said and walked out of the apartment to grab my bag.

"You knew more about Mundy than you let on." His eyes clung to mine.

"You know how I said I questioned the employees at Le Fork?" I asked, but didn't wait for his response. "I've been taking this cake-baking class there." I waved my hand. "Actually, I didn't want to take a class, but I had to distract the store so Jolee could sneak back into the office to get a look at Mundy's file."

"Jolee?" He gasped. "You've dragged her into this?"

"I had to clear my mama." I shot him a look. "I couldn't ask you to do it and we certainly had no time to get a warrant from the Fayette County judge. It was easier for me to sign up for a class and have her look."

"How did she know how to find things?" He wasn't going to let it go. It was the cop in him.

We stalked to the Jeep. I opened the door and pulled my bag out.

I couldn't tell him that my ghost grandfather had gone in and done the work for me and I told Jolee exactly where to look.

"I don't know. She's good at snooping, I guess." I shrugged and headed back inside of the apartment.

"Sheriff," the officer called for me. "We found a note." He held out a piece of paper to me. He had on a glove and handed me one to put on.

I put it on and took the note. I quickly read through it. Mundy had admitted to killing Frank Von Lee because Frank had ruined his career from the beginning. He'd even gone into detail on how much he liked Ben and knew Ben was in financial trouble. He knew Frank was going to try to ruin Ben because that was how Frank was. His life's mission to end Frank Von Lee's career had happened and he no longer wanted to feel the sadness Frank had given him, so he decided to end his life.

"I guess we have our killer." I handed the letter to Finn and let him see it.

"I guess we do." He stared at it for a few minutes before he handed it back to the officer.

"Be sure to get all the paperwork to us." I pulled a business card out of my pocket and handed it to the officer before Finn and I left.

"I'm going to go finish up the paperwork at the department." Finn stood next to his Charger. "Now what?

"I think I'll take the day off since you said you were going to finish up the paperwork." It wasn't a bad suggestion, though I had other plans for him that he didn't need to know about yet. "Why don't you come over for supper?"

"Sounds good." He smiled, bending down to give me a kiss. "I can bring over some good Chicago pizza. My sister sent me some." He kissed me again.

The sound of a click drew us apart. Before I could spot Edna Easterly, I saw the familiar feather disappear through the door of Mundy's apartment but quickly fluttered back out when one of the officers ushered her out. The feather darted back and forth as she tried to explain why she should be there.

"Edna Easterly must live by that police scanner," Finn half joked. "I'll see you tonight. Good job, even though you probably could've used some backup."

"You know that I'm used to doing things on my own. But I'll get better." It was true. I still wasn't used to having to call Finn for backup when it was still so new working together.

I let out a small sigh of relief on my way back into town. A sadness draped over me because I'd not seen Poppa again and I knew that he only showed up during the investigation process of a murder or crime. I'd wished I'd known I was going to find Mundy because I'd have told Poppa goodbye until next time.

I headed to the south side of Cottonwood to Dixon's. I was going to make Finn a cake for tonight. It wasn't going to be refrigerated overnight, but I still had time to let it cool. The excitement of baking a cake coursed through me and I picked up all the stuff I needed.

Too bad Toots wasn't working. I was going to tell her that the murder had been solved and telling her meant the word would get around fast.

The sun suddenly came out as I was leaving. My heart lifted and I held the Dixon's paper bag close to me. I couldn't help but smile thinking that Poppa might've had a hand in the sudden shift of weather. At least that made me feel better about not being able to say goodbye to him.

Chapter Twenty-Nine

"Hey, Riley." I greeted him in the new addition he was working on at Finn's. I tapped the toe of my boot on the hardwood floor. "This looks great. You've done a lot over the past couple of days."

I'd gotten home from Dixon's and immediately started my cake. I put it in the oven and decided to go to Finn's and grab the pizza so he could just come straight to my house after he finished up the paperwork.

His addition was coming along nicely. I didn't know much about construction, but the sheer fact that Danny Shane said Riley Titan wasn't certified could've fooled me. The drywall was all screwed in and the drywall tape had been placed for him to slap on some drywall mud. The wood flooring was a nice dark bamboo.

"He's going to love this bigger family room and so is Cosmo." I couldn't help but smile looking at the ornery cat curled up in the sunspot coming from the new bay window in the addition.

Cosmo had come from another murder investigation. We had to find a home for him. Finn's sister had agreed to take him but quickly realized she was allergic to cats once she'd gotten him back to Chicago. Being the sensitive guy Finn was, he couldn't stand the thought that Cosmo might have to go to a shelter, so he adopted him.

"I barely recognize you out of uniform." He looked me up

and down with my true fashion sense of my sweatshirt and jeans. Not that his paint-splattered plaid shirt and jeans were any better. "What are you doing here?" he asked.

"Do you have an issue with me being here?" I asked.

Cosmo gave a little meow when I walked over to pet him.

"No. Deputy Vincent just said that I'd be here all day alone because he was going to find that chef that made such a ruckus the day that food critic died." He took the drywall spatula and swiped it overtop the drywall tape going down the seam. "That cat doesn't mind all the beating and banging."

"He's sweet." I pulled my hand back when Cosmo got up and arched his back into a big stretch. "Anyways, you do have the work permit, don't you?"

There was a law that any new addition to a structure had to be approved by the council as well as have a permit posted on the window.

"Do you think that Deputy Vincent would let me in here without one?" he asked over his shoulder as he dragged the spatula full of drywall mud down the tape.

"Of course he wouldn't. I'd gone to see Danny Shane and he mentioned that you weren't a registered contractor," I probed.

I took a step back and looked into the finished part of the house. There was a direct line of vision to the front windows where the permit should be posted.

"Aw, he's sore that I'm taking all the business away from him around here since he's been doing bad work." He dropped the spatula to his side and twisted sixty degrees to look at me. "Word gets around Cottonwood fast."

"It sure does." Out of the corner of my eye, Cosmo jumped down from the window ledge. He pranced into the other room followed up by a few meows, which I knew meant he was hungry.

"Kenni." Poppa appeared. "I'm not getting a good feeling

about you being here alone with him."

I gave him a slightly confused look. Why on earth was he here? The murder had been solved. Hadn't it?

"I keep thinking about him." Poppa ghosted next to him. "This job."

I looked around, wondering what Poppa was talking about.

"This was a brand-new addition. Everyone knows that the flooring goes in last." Poppa walked around the perimeter of the room. "Here is drywall mud on the floor. That's one of the reasons the floor goes in last."

"I'm not sure when Finn will be back." Riley threw the spatula in the bucket of drywall mud. His stare was intense. "I'll be sure to tell him that you stopped by."

"I'll call him." I watched his moves. He'd suddenly become uncomfortable. "I've got some new information on the case that gives Chef Mundy an alibi."

"That's good." His eyes narrowed. I could tell he was trying to call my bluff.

"Look there." Poppa pointed to Riley's face. "That's the classic face they teach in the academy."

Reading body language was one of my favorite classes and I did know the look.

"You have to think about all the clues up until now. Everyone knew that Frank Von Lee was coming to town. He suddenly shows up as a contractor and begins to take jobs that can be linked to Frank?" Poppa scratched his chin.

I bit the edge of my lip and looked at Riley, who was staring back at me.

"I'm going to feed Cosmo before I head on out." I gave a slight wave. "Good work. I just might have to hire you." I looked at the floor and noticed more and more dried-up drywall mud.

Out of the corner of my eye, I saw him notice I was looking at the floor. I hurried out of the room. I glanced up to the front of the house. My eyes slid across each window and the front door's window panels to see if there was a posted work permit. There wasn't.

My mind rolled back to the things Poppa had said. Riley showed up at Ben's and put himself in the right place at the right time to talk Ben into hiring him to do that work. Frank was going to be spending a lot of time at the diner. My heart started to beat rapidly when I remembered Riley was at the diner when Mama and Ben had met with Frank alone.

After Frank died, Riley was all of a sudden doing Finn's work, which gives Finn an ear to talk to. Not that Finn would discuss the case, but you never knew what was said over a beer or three.

Then there was the fact that there wasn't a work permit posted at either of the places he'd worked.

Cosmo continually meowed for his food. I slid my glance to the new addition. Riley was still looking at me. I smiled again.

I bent down next to the bag of cat food and pulled out my phone. I quickly scrolled through to Malina's phone number that she'd given me. Quickly I texted her. "Is Riley Titan staying at The Tattered Book Cover and Inn?"

"I don't see a Titan in the register," she texted back.

I used the scoop inside the bag and put two heaping scoops of cat kibble in Cosmo's bowl. While squatted, I glanced over my shoulder through the new door into the addition. Riley's arm was extended in the air, mudding the top of a piece of tape. My eyes drew down the side of his body. His shirt was lifted away from the waist of his jeans. About an inch of his skin was exposed. The metal buckle on his belt caught my attention.

Names on belts as well as needlepoint belts were really popular. Maybe now that Finn and I were on better terms, I'd have a belt or a name plate made for him from Lulu's.

"Kenni." Poppa bent down and looked at the name plate.

"That don't say Titan."

I squinted my eyes.

"It says Tooke. T-o-o-k-e," Poppa read off the letters. "Where have I heard that name before?"

Cosmo smacked his bowl. The food flew across the floor. I scrambled around to pick up a few of the pieces so I could buy some time to figure out what to do with this information. While on my knees, I put my hand in the garbage can to drop the kibble and noticed a couple of frozen meal packages.

Tooke. Frozen meals. Things were beginning to add up. My hands shook. I turned back to Cosmo and reached for him. I had to get him and me out of there. He darted off into the new addition.

I stood up and noticed a wallet on the counter.

"Good boy, Cosmo," I said in order not to draw attention to my snooping. I opened the wallet and pulled out the license just enough to see Riley's photo and the name Riley Tooke.

Tooke was the family's name from the newspaper article I'd read at the library after I'd read Frank Von Lee's biography on the Culinary Channel boasting how Frank was harsh in his reviews and this was what made him so sought after. The article said one of the restaurants that Frank Von Lee had given a bad review was a family-owned restaurant by the Tooke family. A shiver rippled through me.

The family that'd gone bankrupt because of Frank. The same family whose father committed suicide over it. Riley's father. This was the perfect motive for Riley to seek revenge.

If I thought back further, Riley had his ear to the ground when I discussed things. He was at Ben's when the fight went down between Ben and Mundy. That would be perfect for him to pin the murder on Mundy, but why Mama?

"Kenni, let's go. He's going to do something," Poppa predicted. "He's part of that Tooke clan. Now, Kenni," Poppa stressed.

I slid the ID back into the wallet and took out my phone. I had to make sure before I accused him. Not that the frozen dinner, name, and lack of construction knowledge wasn't proof enough that something wasn't right.

"What about the name Tooke?" I quickly texted Malina, ignoring Poppa.

"Yes. Riley Tooke. He's in room six. He's a cutie-pa-tooke." She ended her text with a kissy face emoji. "Get it? Pa-tooke? I talked to him while he made his frozen dinners. Why?"

"Cute but deadly," I whispered.

"So you're trying to figure out exactly how I'm part of this whole Frank Von Lee murder," Riley's voice boomed from behind me.

I jumped, wishing I'd had my gun holster on me. I slid my phone back into my pocket but not without hitting the voice recorder button.

"Too late!" Poppa threw his hands in the air. "I don't get it. I've been runnin' all over hell's half-acre to help you and you just don't listen. Why am I here if you aren't going to listen to me?"

"Excuse me?" I tried to play off Riley's words and scooted closer to the garbage can.

"I'm not stupid. Maybe a little careless, and I underestimated the girly sheriff a little, but I can take care of that." Slowly he tapped the head of a hammer in his palm. "I've got a new job pouring concrete. I really don't know much about it, but I'm sure I can practice digging a hole big enough for a dead body and fill that with concrete."

"You could." I shrugged and glanced around to find anything I could to whack him with before he got me. "Or you can just come clean right now. It's completely understandable how much you wanted to get back at him for bankrupting your family business."

"Bankrupting?" He scoffed. "That's just the tip of the iceberg. He gave our family so much stress, I started drinking more and more. I had a wife and a kid on the way. My parents lost everything and had to move in with us." Tears filled his eyes. His nostrils flared. "I wasn't myself. My parents watched as my marriage drowned because of my drinking. My father said it was his fault for contacting that so-called food critic and just when I thought it couldn't get worse, my dad hung himself."

The pain was so vivid in his mind, his body trembled as he fidgeted with the hammer.

"The judge will hear all of this and I'm sure there will be leniency," I sputtered. "You had all the right in the world to do what you did," I lied. It was the only little bit of hope I had that I could get out of here without a hammer to my head.

"You think I believe you?" He cackled, taking a step forward. "You had me. You really had me."

I took a step back.

"I really didn't know that you knew until you looked at the floor. Then I realized you knew the floor was down first. Rookie mistake," he pointed out.

"Not to mention the frozen food container in the garbage. I did find part of one at Ben's. At first I thought it was Chef Mundy's, but no real chef would ever buy, cook, or eat a frozen dinner." The way I saw it, I might as well throw it all out there so if they found my dead body, I'd have taped the conversation, hoping he wouldn't get away with it. "You bought a frozen pot pie, put the poison in it and made Frank believe it was Mama's pot pie. He bought into it and thought mama sent him the sample the night before the actual tasting. He ate it. He died, making mama look like the killer."

"If you can get into the family room, Finn has a gun in the drawer of the side table of the couch." Poppa disappeared.

I started to slowly edge my way around the kitchen.

"The missing permit signs were also a clue that maybe Danny Shane was right about you not having the right credentials. But the big aha moment..." I slipped around the door jamb and ran down the hall to get to the gun as fast as I could.

"Stop!" He was screaming as his footsteps thundered behind me. "I said stop right there or I'll kill you right here!"

"No! Not if I get you first!" I jerked the drawer open. Nothing. "I thought you said the side table!" I screamed at Poppa's shadow. He stood in front of the window and the afternoon sun was streaming in.

"The other side table." Poppa pointed.

The heavy hand of Riley grabbed me and shoved me. As I was going down, I looked over at Poppa. He disappeared, leaving me a good view of the outside world. Mrs. Brown was standing in Finn's yard with her mouth dropped open.

"I know I can't kill you in Finn's house. I'm going to have to take you to the country." Riley was nodding as he played out the scenario in his head. He shook the butt end of the hammer at me as he gripped the head. "You see, now that Mundy is dead and because of the note I planted, Finn thinks the case is closed. He just left before you got here to do the final report. I kinda like it here. Now that my revenge has been taken care of, I'm ready to live my life as Riley Titan."

He grabbed me by the arm. I winced.

"I can't live that life with you around." He flung me in front of him. "Now we're going to go for a little ride."

If I could keep him here for a few more minutes, I knew Mrs. Brown would get me help. At least I prayed she'd get me help.

"Your belt." I huffed and puffed the words out of my mouth, pointing to his belt. "I recalled reading about your family in an article. Before you kill me, I really need to know how you pulled it off."

"That." He laughed and put the handle of the hammer in his back pocket.

He took off his plaid shirt and ripped it apart in long strips that I could only imagine he was going to use to tie my hands. "I've been waiting for an opportunity for Frank to visit a small town to make my move. After I'd gotten my job with Ben, I listened very carefully and found out where Frank was staying. The media didn't report that. I'd only planned to kill him, but your mama, god bless her heart." He put his hand flat on his chest. "That's what you say around here, right?" He winked.

"Right," I answered sarcastically.

"I had no idea I was going to use her as the scapegoat, but it was perfect. Then Chef Mundy was a bonus. He said he wanted to figure out how to make your mama's pot pie. He loved to figure out secret ingredients. I saw him at the grocery store picking up all sorts of stuff. According to that sweet Malina, who is desperate for a man, Mundy had been cooking the whole time he was there using their oven. It was a perfect set up." He ran his hands through his hair before he gestured me to go closer to the door. "I saw your mama take a casserole dish, so I took a dish from the same pattern and put one of the frozen pot pie dinners in it. After I put a little sodium fluoroacetate in it, I left it on the counter with a note for Malina. Of course I didn't put a name on it. Just that it had to be delivered to Frank Von Lee."

He jerked my arm around and grabbed me by my wrists.

"Now, enough talk. I have to get you out of here before Deputy Vincent gets home," he said.

My heart hammered in my chest as I felt the fabric slide along my wrists. It was times like these that the instructors at the academy warned you that you needed to perform the take out moves as easy as you breathed. I wasn't fond of that class and I didn't memorize all the moves, though now I really wished

I had.

"Hold it right there, buddy," Betty Murphy threatened Riley Titan, Tooke, or whoever he was, my shotgun pointed straight at him. "Don't make me waste a bullet on you."

Mrs. Brown stood behind her with a wooden rolling pin lifted in the air. "I knew he was too cute for a reason. Makes up for his evil insides."

He took his hands off me and put them in the air. I got up and inched around him, taking the gun from Betty.

"How did you know I was here?" I asked Betty.

"Mrs. Brown called me and I knew I could get here quicker than Finn." Betty and Mrs. Brown high-fived. "He'd made a detour to grab a bite to eat before he came to finish up the paperwork on Mundy."

"Betty, can you run down to my Jeep and grab my police bag?" I asked.

Without a word, she high-tailed it out of Finn's house.

I kept the shotgun on Tooke and pulled my phone out with the other hand. I turned off the voice recording and noticed the time. I was going to be a little late to finish my cake. I messaged the recordings to Finn's phone, and then I called the reserve office telling them to send someone to Free Row and haul the real murderer off to jail.

"You got this until the reserve officer comes?" I asked Betty after I'd securely cuffed Tooke by the hands and feet and noticed the time.

"You're leaving?" she asked with fear in her eyes and took the shotgun when I handed it to her.

"Yep. I have a cake to finish baking and I need to check on it." I brushed my hands together and took one last look at Tooke all cuffed up.

"About that." Mrs. Brown's voice faded away. "There was smoke coming from the backyard and I went over to make sure everything was okay. Your cake."

"Yeah." I lifted my head to listen.

"It's burnt." Mrs. Brown's nose crunched up. "To a crisp. I figured you were down here so that's when I came down to get you. I saw through the window what was going on."

Thank God for nosy neighbors.

Chapter Thirty

"It's not an original Kenni Lowry cake, but I guess it'll do." I forked a big piece of Ben's hot fudge brownie pie with a big scoop of vanilla ice cream and fed it across the table to Finn.

"I still can't believe you're taking a cake-baking class." He smiled and my heart beat double time. He got up from his side of the table and came over to sit in the seat next to me. He slipped his arm around my shoulder, picked up a spoon, and fed me a bite.

"It was for the good of the badge." I winked, tilting my head up to kiss him. I dropped my chin on his shoulder with a sigh of pleasure. "It feels so good to have Frank's death behind us."

"I knew something was wrong when I read Mundy's letter. It didn't seem authentic. I'd even gone back to Ben's on my way back to the office to finish the report and he told me that he never discussed finances with Mundy. He mentioned it in passing to Riley after he and Danny Shane had his blow up. That's what made me head on out to Danny's and talk to him. He told me that he told you Riley didn't have the proper certification. Things started to fit together after that." He scooped another big bite with a lot of fudge. He held it up to my lips and I happily accepted it. "I called dispatch to let Betty know I was going to head home to confront Riley about his work and she didn't answer. I also wanted her to read the rest of the lab results to me. I took it upon myself to call the lab and he told me that Mundy's prints weren't on anything in Frank's evidence.

He said all the blood from Mundy's room and knives you'd taken in as evidence only had chicken and his own blood on it. He pulled one print from Frank's room. He ran the print in the database and it belonged to Riley Tooke."

"He had a record?" That was new to me.

"He'd been picked up for shoplifting as a kid and his print was still on file." He took his arm from around me. He leaned against the table and rested on his forearms. "I made a quick call to the reserves and they pulled his name and photo. It was Riley Titan."

"He was smart. He positioned himself everywhere Frank would be and Mundy would be. Even staying in the same inn as both." I couldn't believe that it took us this long to solve it, but Riley was smart.

The bell over the diner door dinged. For a second it dawned on me that maybe it was Poppa with his real ding and not him mocking me. When I turned around, I saw it was the next best thing.

Mama.

"You ain't gonna believe this." She waved a magazine in the air. "I'm famous!"

She smacked the magazine in front of me and Finn opened to the page she wanted me to see. She jabbed it.

"I'm in here." She pointed to one of the photos that Edna had taken of her in the diner that morning before all this mess had happened.

"That's fantastic." I stood up and gave my mama a huge hug.

"Is that it?" Ben walked over and pointed to the magazine.

"It is." Mama took out a piece of paper from her purse. "And I want you to have this."

"What is it?" He opened it. "It's a check." His jaw dropped.

"That should be enough to buy this old run-down building."

Mama hugged Ben. "I told the magazine that I knew they were going to make a big documentary on Frank's life and death and if they wanted my interview they had to pay me. Pay me good." She nodded.

"Mama, you never cease to amaze me." I drew her into a big bear hug. Ben grabbed both of us.

"Now get off me. I've got to show people how famous I am." She pulled away from us and darted over to a group of the Sweet Adelines, bragging on herself.

Ben rushed back to the counter where Jolee was helping him. By the look on her face, they were happy he'd be able to keep the diner.

"Are you okay?" Finn asked.

I looked around the diner. Mama was walking around showing the full diner her famous spread. I could see Jolee and Ben joking around with each other from behind the counter. And a warm arm had slipped around me.

"I'm more than okay." I looked up at my devilishly handsome boyfriend. "Life is just about perfect. Everyone I love is happy and healthy."

"Are you saying you love me?" Finn whispered in my ear. My body tingled.

I gulped. My palms started to sweat and my mouth suddenly went dry.

"Because I love you."

His words were music to my ears.

TONYA KAPPES

Tonya has written over 20 novels and 4 novellas, all of which have graced numerous bestseller lists including *USA Today*. Best known for stories charged with emotion and humor, and filled with flawed characters, her novels have garnered reader praise and glowing critical reviews. She lives with her husband, three teenage boys, two very spoiled schnauzers and one ex-stray cat in Kentucky.

**The Kenni Lowry Mystery Series
by Tonya Kappes**

FIXIN' TO DIE (#1)
SOUTHERN FRIED (#2)
AX TO GRIND (#3)
SIX FEET UNDER (#4)
DEAD AS A DOORNAIL (#5)

BALTIMORE COUNTY
PUBLIC LIBRARY

CPSIA information can be obtained
at www.ICGtesting.com
Printed in the USA
LVHW02s0114160518
577269LV00022B/219/P